THE UNFORGIVING EYE

Returning from their honeymoon, John and Lydia Savidge are offered an extraordinary challenge: they are given three days to discover who killed Sir Benedict Stanbury, master of Fallowfield. Could the hapless stable hand accused of the crime really be guilty? Perhaps it was Sir Benedict's hoydenish niece or her mercenary mama? Or could it have been the suspicious solicitor or the frightened governess? Almost everyone had a motive for murder, but nobody can provide an alibi. Lydia and John have to unravel the tangled skein of perverse relationships and eccentric personalities before the startling truth is finally revealed.

Beth Andrews has been an avid reader since childhood, and her love of the Regency period began when she read her first Georgette Heyer novel in the 1970s. She has also written *Hidden in the Heart*. Beth lives in the Bahamas.

BETH ANDREWS

THE UNFORGIVING EYE

Complete and Unabridged

ULVERSCROFT
Leicester

First published in Great Britain in 2008 by
Robert Hale Limited
London

First Large Print Edition
published 2009
by arrangement with
Robert Hale Limited
London

British Library CIP Data

Andrews, Beth.
    The unforgiving eye
    1. Great Britain- -History- -Geoge III, *1760 – 1820*- -
Fiction. 2. Detective and mystery stories.
    3. Large type books.
    I. Title
    813.6–dc22

    ISBN 978–1–84782–664–0

Published by
F. A. Thorpe (Publishing)
Anstey, Leicestershire

Set by Words & Graphics Ltd.
Anstey, Leicestershire
Printed and bound in Great Britain by
T. J. International Ltd., Padstow, Cornwall

This book is printed on acid-free paper

For Jackie and Tony,
not necessarily because
you remind me of Lydia and John,
but just because.

'An unforgiving eye
and a damned disinheriting countenance!'

The School for Scandal
(Act IV, Scene I)
Richard Brinsley Sheridan

The Beginning

England, 1818

Slipping noiselessly out of the side door, Portia drew the folds of her bottle-green cloak about her. She made sure to keep close to any convenient bush or tree which might provide a measure of concealment, moving cautiously but steadily away from the great house, looking back occasionally to ascertain that no one followed.

The full moon was like a silver-gilt quizzing glass in the sky above, and she could almost imagine the eye of God glaring down at her through its glowing circle. That the Deity would disapprove of her intentions was beyond question. There was a time when she herself would have trembled at the very thought of such things. But she had long since gained supremacy over her conscience, and she crushed it ruthlessly now, feeling scarcely a twinge of doubt or remorse. Not

1

for her the timidity or hesitation of other young ladies! No. She was mistress of her own destiny, whatever might be the consequences.

The house was already a good distance behind her, and she heaved a sigh of relief, emerging from the shadows on to a large expanse of lawn — a sea of dull grey beneath her slippered feet. It was unlikely that anyone would see her here. She was alone . . . or almost. Was that the crunch of footsteps nearby?

'James!' she called in a loud whisper — and even that sound, slight as it was, seemed magnified ten-fold in the silence.

There was no answer. She must have imagined it. On a night like this, it was easy for one's mind to play such tricks. Or perhaps her conscience was not as moribund as she assumed. No matter.

She had not much further to go. The bulk of the temple was clearly visible through the stand of ash trees, but no light from within yet illumined its windows of stained glass.

Suddenly there was another sound. Unlike her hesitant voice a few moments before, this brought her abruptly to a halt, her eyes widening in instant fear and disbelief. It was a sound at once familiar and incongruous. Loud, angry, threatening, it was completely out of place in so tranquil a setting.

'Good God!' she muttered under her breath. Unless she was mistaken, it had come from the direction of the temple itself.

She had been walking briskly, but now she hitched up her skirts in her clenched fingers and ran headlong towards the building, her mind struggling to make some connection between that terrible sound and her own clandestine mission. Surely it could not be what it seemed.

Swift as her progress was, her heart galloped so frantically within her breast that it seemed almost as if it would arrive there before her. With her eyes fixed on the open door of the building in front of her, Portia did not notice a shadow half-hidden by shrubbery running swiftly away almost parallel to her but in the opposite direction.

Her thought — her fear — was what she might find waiting inside the temple. Indeed, she could scarcely say *what* she expected. Some instinct warned her of evil to come, but she had no idea of the fate which lurked in the gloom beyond . . .

1

If Wishes Were Murders

'I am not in the humour for murder, Lydia.'

'Why ever not?'

John Savidge glanced down at his wife, who was seated beside him in the carriage as it bumped and battled its way along the rutted roads of Hertfordshire. Her cheeks, framed by a Coburg bonnet of vivid carmine, were flushed, and her eyes bright with excitement. One might almost be forgiven for thinking her pretty at that moment. He smiled indulgently.

'You cannot forgive me for depriving you of the pleasure of sniffing out a killer?'

'It is like depriving a hound of hunting a fox,' she complained. She countered this, however, by leaning against him in a familiar and comfortable manner. 'And I still say that Hampshire was not so very far out of our way.'

'Have the first weeks of our marriage been so very dull, my dear?' He pulled her closer, his right arm about her shoulders.

'By no means!' she declared emphatically. 'But a nice little murder would have been just the thing to make it absolutely perfect.'

'I fear that we must settle for something rather less than perfection,' he said against her ear.

'You are right, of course,' she conceded, stifling a giggle at the tickling sensation caused by his breath. 'We must discharge our duty to Mrs Wardle-Penfield, after all.'

'I would not dare return to Sussex without obeying her request.'

'It was more in the nature of a decree.'

They both laughed at this, though it was no less than the truth. Mrs Wardle-Penfield was more likely to command than to solicit a favour. In this case it was a simple enough errand, and one which they could hardly refuse, since she had been condescending enough to provide them with her own carriage for their bridal trip. The lady had, of course, been perfectly aware of the obligation under which this placed them. That was undoubtedly part of the charm in her scheme.

'It surely cannot be much further?' Lydia wondered aloud as a sudden jolt reminded her afresh that the old coach was not so well sprung as newer conveyances were.

'Well,' John shifted his rather imposing frame a little and peered out of the window, 'we passed through Ware about half an hour ago, and it is a distance of only a few miles to Fallowfield.'

Lydia was not really much interested in Fallowfield, though she was told that the house was large and the grounds quite out of the common way. They had already seen the chief spectacles of Hertfordshire, including Hatfield House, and she did not expect that their present destination would eclipse that monumental pile with its Long Room which Lydia felt could have hosted a decent indoor horse race. The only reason for this detour on their return journey was the fact that the inhabitants of the house included Mrs Wardle-Penfield's goddaughter, Portia Leverett, and Portia's mother, who had been a bosom-bow of Mrs W.P. in their school days. Portia had only recently achieved her majority, and her godmother had instructed the newlyweds to take just an extra hour or two to present her with a letter and a small gift in token of the momentous occasion.

It was some time before they found the road which led to Fallowfield. Nevertheless, it was not quite noon when they drew up before the commodious residence. It was a somewhat monotonous Palladian house, very square and plain, with four Doric columns flanking the portico. Attractive enough, perhaps, but somewhat unimaginative. One saw such buildings everywhere, and was glad to turn one's eyes to the irregular dwellings of a country village, with their thatched roofs, rough stone and beams just a trifle askew.

It was plain that the family must be one of considerable wealth and standing, however. Mrs Wardle-Penfield would not allow anything else in someone she condescended to acknowledge as a godchild.

Their coachman opened the door and John descended before helping his wife down after him. In her hand she clutched the small parcel, neatly wrapped and tied with stout cord.

Together they approached the large front door, which was opened even before they could knock. Apparently someone had been on the watch for their arrival — though Lydia did not think that their visit had been announced beforehand.

A well-built man of middling age — obviously the butler — greeted them in a politely subdued manner and listened quietly to their explanation of why they were come into this part of the country.

'If you would be so kind as to wait in the drawing-room here,' he suggested, directing them through an open door on their right, 'I will summon Miss — '

'Who is it, Jenkins?' a rather flute-like female voice interrupted him, and Lydia and John turned about to encounter a vision — or, more accurately, an apparition.

Coming towards them, seeming to float rather than walk, was a figure arrayed entirely in black crêpe, her face almost completely concealed behind a veil of the same hue. Lydia almost gasped at this alarmingly dramatic entrance, while John stared at the woman in a mixture of surprise and disbelief.

'It's a Mr and Mrs Savidge, ma'am,' Jenkins answered. 'They've come with a little summat from Miss Portia's godmother.'

With a swift, fluid gesture, the dark lady lifted her veil to reveal a face of somewhat faded beauty. She was a woman of between forty and fifty years, still well preserved and with an obvious taste for theatrics.

'Ah!' she cried. 'Dear Hermione! So thoughtful. She does not know — she could never have guessed, of course . . . '

Her voice trailed off, leaving the cryptic words hanging in the air of the hall like a verbal fog.

'Forgive us for intruding, ma'am,' Lydia ventured hopefully. 'You are obviously in mourning.'

9

'Ah yes!' The words were spoken tremulously, while a black handkerchief was pressed to brimming eyes as a token of silent suffering.

'A member of the family, ma'am?'

'My brother-in-law, sir,' the lady confirmed. 'A man still in the prime of life . . . so handsome too . . . such a fine figure . . . '

Her voice trailed off again. She seemed all but overcome by her emotions and actually leaned against the wall.

'You were very fond of your brother-in-law, Mrs . . . ?' Now it was Lydia's voice which died away when she realized that they were still quite unaware of the lady's identity.

'How remiss of me!' The funereal dame declared, momentarily forgetting her indulgence in grief. 'I am Mrs Leverett. The gift which you have so kindly brought to us is for my daughter, Portia.'

'It is unfortunate that we should have arrived at so awkward a moment,' John asserted, ready to back out of the house as quickly as possible.

'But that is no reason for a lack of hospitality, sir.' Mrs Leverett's air was one of studied languor, so her protest could hardly be described as decisive. Nevertheless, it was plain that she intended for them to remain for the moment, if not for their sakes then for the sake of her reputation as a hostess.

After a brief consultation with the butler, she directed them into a large apartment hung with gold damask curtains and generally displaying an impressive opulence. Once they were all seated, however, a depressing silence descended upon them as nobody could think of anything insipid enough with which to begin a conversation. At last Lydia spoke.

'Had your brother-in-law been ill for very long?'

Lydia's question, while not impolite, smacked as much of curiosity as concern, and John frowned very slightly. Mrs Leverett was not at all offended. Quite the reverse, in fact. She was enjoying her role too much.

'Ill!' The word would seem to be quite foreign to her. 'I dare say Benedict never suffered a day's illness in his life. He had a remarkable constitution.'

'Sir Benedict's death was quite sudden, quite unexpected then?'

John did not like the direction in which this was leading. He could already see by the way that his wife leaned forward, her body tense and her eyes blazing, that Lydia was all too eager to believe that the master of Fallowfield had met his untimely end by means most unnatural. He could almost read the thoughts parading wantonly through her head, and guessed that she was pondering what kind of poison might effect a quick exit from this world into the next.

If Lydia suspected poison, however, she was quickly disabused of this idea from a quite unexpected source. While Mrs Leverett was commanding their full attention, a fourth member had been added to their small circle. She stood in the entrance to the drawing-room and made her presence known by answering Lydia's question in a tone which was at once loud and perfectly void of any emotion.

'My uncle's death was not merely unexpected; it was quite shocking,' she announced, adding for their benefit, 'He was shot through the head, you see.'

2

An Unexpected Invitation

'Portia!' Mrs Leverett leaned back in her chair as though she was preparing to join her late brother-in-law in the Next World. 'Have you no sense of decorum?'

'It is not exactly a secret, Mama,' the young lady retorted. She advanced into the room, and Lydia saw that she was a tall girl, not precisely a classical beauty but one who would undoubtedly be admired by gentlemen with a discerning eye. Her figure was excellent, she moved gracefully but with purpose, and there was a force of personality about her which reminded Lydia more of Mrs Wardle-Penfield than it did of Mrs Leverett. Perhaps the most striking thing about her, however, was her ensemble. She was dressed in a morning gown of pink-and-white, with not even a hint of black about her. A spencer jacket, also in pink, indicated that she had been out of doors — a conjecture further enhanced by her matching cheeks.

Her mother might be the absolute caricature of a mourning relation, but Miss Leverett was the picture of gay unconcern.

'My uncle,' she repeated, disposing herself comfortably in a large armchair, 'was shot to death four days ago.'

'And still you have not enough respect for his memory to dress appropriately!'

This was from her mother, who cast a despairing glance at her offspring. Perhaps, Lydia considered, the daughter felt that her mother was wearing enough black for two.

'Why should I pretend to mourn for Uncle Benedict?' Portia asked reasonably. 'I found him insufferable in life, and he continues to vex us even in death.'

This point of view was clearly one not shared by her mama, who tried to turn the conversation before her daughter could say anything more outrageous.

'I'm afraid,' she said, 'that I have been remiss in my duties. I have not introduced you to our guests, my dear.'

She immediately remedied this lapse. The effect upon her daughter was quite unexpected, however.

'Mr and Mrs John Savidge!' Miss Leverett cried, almost vaulting from her seat. 'Can it be? Can it really be true?'

'You have heard of us, Miss Leverett?' John

enquired, uncertain whether to be flattered or alarmed by her evident joy.

'You are even younger than I had imagined from my godmother's description.'

'Mrs Wardle-Penfield has told you of us?' Lydia asked in some surprise.

'She wrote to me some weeks ago. Do you not remember, Mama, what I told you of the murder in the woods near Diddlington?'

Mrs Leverett acknowledged that she did vaguely recall some tale of the kind. The names of the parties involved escaped her memory.

Portia then regaled her with a reasonably accurate rendering of the story, with which John and Lydia were all too well acquainted.

'Heavens!' the older woman announced at the end. 'What very unpleasant persons seem to inhabit your village.'

'But this is wonderful! Quite wonderful!' her daughter beamed upon them, ignoring her comment.

'It is?' John was not certain that he liked the direction in which this was heading.

'Oh indeed, sir!' Portia Leverett said emphatically. 'Were I not an avowed atheist, I would almost swear that it was the hand of Divine Providence.'

'Would you?' Lydia stared at her with some misgiving.

'You must — you simply must remain here and discover who it was that murdered my uncle.'

There was a moment of silence as her three listeners considered this artless statement. It was John who finally found his voice.

'My dear Miss Leverett,' he said, frowning at her with as stern a countenance as he could muster, 'we came here solely to deliver a gift from your godmother. We must be getting back to Sussex as soon as possible.'

'Nonsense!' The young lady clearly thought his argument unworthy of consideration. 'I will have your baggage brought in at once, and my godmother's carriage and cattle will easily find accommodation in the stables.'

'How long do you intend for us to remain here?' Lydia demanded. She was not averse to hunting murderers. In fact, it had been barely an hour ago that she had been wishing for just such an opportunity. But she found this high-handed treatment disconcerting and, frankly, annoying.

'It will not be long, I am sure, before you have discovered the solution to this vexatious mystery.'

'Mystery!' Mrs Leverett interjected at this point. 'There is no mystery here, Portia. Benedict's killer has already been apprehended.'

This pronouncement did not suit her daughter, who turned on her with such ferocity that Lydia was quite startled.

'James is innocent! I will not have you saying otherwise, do you hear me!'

'Someone has already been charged with the crime?' John asked calmly.

'One of the stable hands,' Mrs Leverett answered dismissively.

'It's a lie!' Portia cried, only slightly less intense than before. 'James never killed anyone. He is incapable of doing such a thing.'

'You had best leave things well enough alone, girl,' Portia's mother said grimly, forgetting her grief-stricken pose. 'No good will come of this. Mark my words.'

'Will you help me?'

Insensible of her mother's arguments, Portia looked from Lydia to John, and her tone of entreaty was not to be denied. It was one thing to object to coercion, and quite another to deny a heartfelt plea for justice.

'Perhaps we could remain here for a few days,' John conceded.

'Shall we say three days?' Portia suggested. 'That should be sufficient, should it not?'

'Very well.'

It was an absurdly brief span of time, Lydia thought. Whether John believed them up to the challenge, or whether he simply wanted to get home as quickly as possible, she could not decide.

'We cannot promise anything, of course,' she hastened to warn the other girl. 'We have had some small success in the past, but — '

'I commend your modesty, Mrs Savidge.' Portia brightened at once. 'However, I have every faith in your abilities. Mrs Wardle-Penfield speaks very highly of your character and your intellect, and I am confident that you will be able to discover the truth and save James from the gibbet.'

★ ★ ★

'Do you think that we are doing the right thing, John?'

'I am surprised to hear you ask such a question. After all, is this not somewhat in the nature of an answer to your prayers?'

'For a man to be murdered!' she cried indignantly. 'I should say not.'

They were ensconced in a very commodious bedchamber, having had their belongings removed from the carriage and taken up but a few minutes before. The room was on the corner of the house, well lit with windows on two sides. Lydia was lying upon the rose-shaded damask counterpane which covered the bed, but at this she sat upright and looked accusingly at her unrepentant spouse.

'Perhaps not precisely that,' he said, depositing himself beside her with his boots dangling over the opposing side of the bed. 'But you certainly had murder in mind as we were driving hither.'

'How wicked I must be.'

'To own the truth,' he returned, neither contradicting nor accusing her, 'I cannot help but be intrigued by this.'

'I knew it!'

Lydia felt a surge of triumph. John might be annoyingly phlegmatic about the whole thing, but she knew him to be every bit as determined as she could be.

'What do you make of Miss Leverett?' he asked her now.

'A very independent-minded young lady, I should say.'

'Who will soon become excessively tire-some,' he concluded.

'That may be *your* opinion.'

'It will be yours by and by.'

She chose to ignore this, merely asking, 'What if we do not succeed?'

'Then Miss Portia is like to be very cross.'

'That, I imagine, is putting it mildly.'

They both lay in silence for a few moments. Though they had been married for little more than a fortnight, Lydia fancied that she could pretty much guess her husband's thoughts. Like her, he was more concerned with the question of whether or not Portia's suspicions were correct. Was the man accused of the crime truly innocent? If so, then the question which followed was this: was someone at Fallowfield a murderer?

'We had better begin at once.'

John rose from the bed with surprising agility for one of his mammoth stature. Lydia immediately followed his example.

'Where do we begin?' she enquired, glancing at her reflection in a conveniently placed mirror and carefully smoothing her mouse-coloured locks into place.

'At the beginning, I suppose.'

★　★　★

Descending to the ground floor of the house, they presently found Miss Leverett where they had left her in the drawing-room. Her mother had vanished, as befitted an apparition of her stature.

'Miss Leverett,' John said, coming straight to the point, 'would you be so good as to show us in which room your uncle was slain?'

The young lady blinked at the two Savidges

20

confronting her with such businesslike determination.

'You are certainly wasting no time, sir,' she
said with some surprise, though not without
approbation.

'If an innocent man's life hangs in the
balance,' Lydia reminded her, 'there is surely
no time to be lost.'

'Very true, ma'am.'

'Then, if it is not distasteful to you, will you
conduct us to the chamber in question?'

'Naturally.' She turned on her heel and
preceded them out of the room. 'I will
conduct you to the temple directly.'

'Temple?' Lydia cried, mystified.

'Yes indeed. My uncle was not killed in the
house, you understand.'

'Was he not?'

Lydia and John exchanged glances. Their
enquiry was just beginning, and already they
had made unfounded assumptions. Their
patroness — if such she could be termed
— led them down the hallway and towards
the rear of the building, explaining that they
must traverse the grounds of Fallowfield in
order to find the spot where Sir Benedict had
expired.

The park surrounding the house was quite
extensive, and laid out in the true English
style, with rolling lawns of fresh green grass

and trees and shrubbery planted in a manner precisely designed to give the impression of being perfectly natural and unplanned.

Fallowfield House itself was set on rising ground, with the drive to the front door being on the lower portion, while the ground rose up gradually behind it. A series of gravel paths wound their way through hedges and miniature groves, until one reached the top of the hillock, beyond the crest of which the land fell away in a series of terraces down to a small lake.

Almost at the edge of the lake was an oddly constructed building whose indigestible architecture was reflected in the tranquil waters. Hexagonal in design, it was topped by a ribbed dome surmounted by a small statue of some kind. Each side of the structure had either a door or window with a pointed arch in the style of Early English architecture. The whole was surrounded by a covered porch supported by Ionic columns.

'The Temple of the Seven Virtues,' Miss Leverett explained when they eventually paused a few yards away from the entrance.

Now that they were near enough to examine the structure, they could see that there were four large windows and two doors at opposite ends of the building. The windows were adorned with fanciful stained glass in vibrant colours which completely obscured any view of the interior.

'This is where your uncle was murdered?' Lydia asked.

'It is.'

'Was his . . . body . . . discovered within the temple, or outside?'

'Just inside the door.'

She stepped forward and flung open the door as she spoke. It opened inwards with only the slightest of creaks and they stared into the dimly lit interior.

It was oddly furnished, to be sure. In the centre of the room was what looked like a baptismal font: a pillar or plinth of carved stone perhaps four feet in height. Along the angled walls were thickly cushioned seats or benches — or, more accurately, sofas, as they were almost three feet deep. Above them, carved wooden beams supported the peaked roof beneath the dome. The floor was decorated in mosaics representing various plants and fruits.

'The stained-glass windows,' she intoned in the manner of a disinterested guide, 'depict the four cardinal virtues of justice, wisdom, courage and moderation.'

There were two doors on opposite sides of the building. Only one set of doors was ever used, however: the opposing doors were locked. Above the entrance was a circular window depicting an empty tomb, which symbolized the theological virtue of faith; and above the exit was a dove, which supposedly represented hope. Miss Leverett explained that the dome was crowned with the figure of Eros.

'Eros?' Lydia could not resist asking.

'The god of love,' the other girl answered with a soulful sigh.

'Most inappropriate — but not entirely unexpected.'

Portia seemed surprised. 'But is not love the greatest of all virtues?'

'Undoubtedly.' John smiled slightly. 'However, it is Caritas rather than Eros which Christian sages have extolled.'

'Caritas?' It was Portia's turn to be mystified.

'Charity. I believe the Greek term is *agape*,' John said with a certain air of conscious superiority. 'It is the sacrificial love of Christ, quite different from the sensuality of Eros — or Venus.'

Portia shrugged, bored by philosophical precision. Lydia eyed her husband with growing respect. She had not suspected him of so much erudition. Apparently, some stray bits of his classical education had unintentionally been retained in his mind.

'So this is where Sir Benedict died . . . ' Lydia said at last.

'In the exact spot where I now stand,' the young lady agreed. 'You may still see a small bloodstain here by the font.'

'Who found him?' John asked.

'I did,' she answered calmly.

Lydia had been staring at Miss Leverett's feet, trying to imagine the body of the master of Fallowfield lying there. At this, however, she looked up. Surely one would expect the girl to display some emotion at such a scene. Lydia could discern nothing in the young lady's countenance, however. She appeared perfectly indifferent.

'Would you be so good as to tell me precisely what happened, Miss Leverett?'

She showed no hesitation in recounting the events of that evening. She had, she said, been making her way towards the temple when she heard the sound of a gun being fired. Certain that it had come from the temple itself, she ran towards it. The door was open but the night was too dark for her to see very much at first. Indeed, she had not realized that her uncle's body was lying just within the aperture until she quite literally tripped over it as she advanced. She would have fallen on her face, had she not clutched at the door handle to steady herself.

At first she thought it must have been James. Bending closer, however, she quickly ascertained that it was indeed Sir Benedict. His eyes were wide open and there was a rather ghastly hole in his temple, from which a fair amount of blood was oozing. She could detect no breathing, and concluded that her uncle was dead.

All this she related in a tone as devoid of expression as her description of the stained glass had been.

'And you saw no one else?' John asked.

'No one.'

'At what hour was this?'

'I cannot say precisely,' she confessed, 'but I believe it was almost a half-hour after midnight.'

'After midnight!' Lydia was surprised into imprudent speech. 'My dear Miss Leverett, what were you doing wandering about the grounds at that hour?'

'I was going to meet James, of course.'

'Going to meet a servant at midnight!'

'James is far more to me than a mere servant,' the amazing Miss Leverett replied. 'He is my lover.'

3

Love and Other Follies

'In fact,' Portia continued, tipping them a doubler, 'I am carrying his child.'

'Carrying . . . ' Lydia could say no more, but merely stared at the girl before her as if she were some improbable heroine from an Italian opera.

'Did you often meet the stable hand here at the temple?' John enquired, no more perturbed than if he were asking her whether she often played piquet.

'Three or four nights each week.'

'It appears that your uncle must have learned of your . . . liaison . . . and meant to confront you here that night.'

'That is my supposition.'

'You were unaware of his intentions?'

Her head turned sharply, a look of anger flashing in her eyes.

'Are you suggesting that James and I knew that he would be there, and — and . . . ?' Her voice trailed off, as if she could not bring

r to speak the words.
It is certainly within the realm of possibility.'

'Do you really believe that I would have asked you to find my uncle's killer, if I had committed the deed myself?'

'It would be a clever way to divert suspicion from yourself,' Lydia pointed out.

Portia was in a fine dudgeon now.

'I would never permit the man I love — the father of my unborn child — to hang for my misdeeds!' she cried nobly. 'If that is the best you can do, sir, perhaps I have been mistaken in asking for your help.'

'If,' John informed her, 'you desire to learn the truth, Miss Leverett, then you must allow us to explore every avenue in order to find it, however unpleasant or unflattering it may be. We know nothing of you or your family, after all.'

His plain speaking disconcerted her for a moment, but she recovered quickly and expressed a reluctant admiration. Here was clearly someone who was not so easily browbeaten.

'Very well,' she conceded at last.

'Do you know of anyone who particularly disliked your uncle?' Lydia asked.

'Everyone who ever met him, I imagine.' She paused a moment, considering. 'Except for poor Winny.'

'Winny?'

'Lawrence Chetwin,' she explained. 'He shares the house with us. His late father had been steward of the estate.'

'He was a friend of Sir Benedict?'

'His only friend, I would say. Fanatically devoted to him since they were boys. It is quite incomprehensible. Which is not to say that Winny is the most agreeable of men, but Uncle Benedict was perfectly beastly.'

It seemed that Mr Chetwin had saved the other man's life when they were children and Sir Benedict had fallen through the ice-encrusted pond. They had served in the army together, fighting against the turncoat Americans, which only strengthened the early bond between them.

'Poor Winny.' She shook her head, not so much in sadness as in a kind of amused contempt. 'He was completely shattered when I told him what had happened. Really, he might almost have been a corpse himself, and declared that it could not be so, that I must have been mistaken. It took me some time to convince him, indeed.'

'I suppose,' Lydia could not refrain from mentioning, 'that there is no possibility that your uncle might have taken his own life?'

Portia shook her head in a decided negative. The idea, she said, was absurd in the extreme. Sir Benedict was not the kind of man to quit this world while there were still victims enough for him to torment. Besides, it so happened that the gun from which the fatal shot was fired was not lying beside the body but had been found two days afterwards along a path leading back towards the house. It was unlikely that anyone could shoot themselves in the head and then fling the weapon several hundred yards away before expiring.

'We may therefore dismiss one theory at least,' John said.

'If you wish to see the gun,' Portia told him, 'it is in my uncle's study. It was one of a matched pair of pistols which my uncle had made some years ago.'

'Manton's?' John inquired.

'No,' she answered. 'I believe they were made by Mr Mortimer.'

'Excellent quality.' John nodded sagely.

Lydia, not being conversant with the intricacies of pistol manufacturing, was somewhat lost. Nevertheless, she could not help but wonder at the irony of a man being killed by one of his own firearms.

'The gun,' she said, 'must have been stolen from his study.'

'Yes. But everyone knew where the pistols were kept,' Portia added, 'and anyone could have taken them that night, or before. I do not suppose that even my uncle could remember the last time they were ever used.'

'Tell me, Miss Leverett,' John said, looking around again at the shadowed temple, 'is there anything . . . unusual . . . that you can recollect about that evening?'

She paused for a moment before responding, 'Nothing that I can recall, sir.'

'Think carefully about it,' he instructed her, 'and if anything, however trivial, should occur to you, I would appreciate it if you would inform me at once.'

'Certainly.' She stepped back into the afternoon sunshine. 'Shall we return to the house?'

'I think that Mrs Savidge and I will remain here a while longer,' he said.

'Very well.' She shrugged. 'I will see you both at supper.'

'And perhaps afterwards we will have a look at your uncle's study.'

*　*　*

For a time after her departure, John and Lydia remained silent. Each was lost in their own private thoughts while they slowly made their way along the path which encircled the ornamental lake. Every so often a stray leaf would drift down from the trees as they shed their foliage in preparation for the coming winter. Only the crunch-crunch of their feet upon the gravel and the whisper of the wind disturbed the tranquillity of the scene.

Eventually they arrived at the point directly opposite the temple and gazed upon it from the farther shore. At this distance, it did not look quite so ungainly, and its reflection in the still waters of the lake was pleasant enough.

'The Temple of the Seven Virtues,' Lydia mused aloud.

'Something of a misnomer, you are thinking?'

'It seems to have inspired anything but virtue.'

'Unless we consider Sir Benedict's death an act of justice, perhaps?'

'Do you suspect Miss Leverett?' she asked bluntly.

'Of course I do.' He smiled down at her. 'Until I learn more, I am inclined to suspect everyone.'

'I suppose it could not have been a stranger . . . '

He gave her a look which indicated that this was nonsense. It was most unlikely that a stranger could have gained access to Fallowfield, stolen the pistol and waylaid the master of the house on the night in question.

'We must waste no time, Lydia,' John said decisively. 'I do not wish to delay our return to Sussex any longer than is necessary.'

It was determined that they would begin by inspecting Sir Benedict's office that very evening. What they might find there was beyond any conjecture. It might yield nothing at all of value. Following that, they must begin by questioning each inhabitant of Fallowfield House concerning the events of the fateful day.

'I think it best if you speak with the ladies — except for Miss Leverett, of course.'

'Who might not be considered precisely a lady?' she suggested somewhat maliciously.

'She is certainly a very headstrong female.'

'She does not open her mouth, but what something quite astonishing comes out of it.'

He chuckled. 'Be careful, my dear. You begin to sound like Mrs Wardle-Penfield. A staid married lady already!'

'If you mean to insult me, sir,' she replied with great dignity, 'perhaps we should return to the house.'

'Did I not tell you that you would soon weary of Miss Portia?'

'I am not precisely weary,' she contradicted. 'But I am certainly inclined to pity the poor stable hand. I do not doubt that she set her cap at him merely to infuriate her uncle! I can well imagine her commanding him to seduce her.'

'Oh no,' he protested. 'Her passion for him seems quite genuine.'

'Rather excessive, I should say. In her own way, she is as much addicted to histrionics as her mama.'

'You do not approve of Miss Leverett's base-born lover?'

'His birth is not the issue, as well you know.'

'She seems to care little for her reputation,' he mused.

'Indeed, she seems intent upon throwing it away.'

'You would never have permitted *me* such liberties before our marriage.' His eyes twinkled with mischief.

'*You* would never have behaved in such a fashion to me,' she said confidently. 'I remember a certain evening in Wickham Wood when you had every opportunity to do so.'

'But had I attempted to go beyond a kiss?' He raised an eyebrow suggestively.

'Then I assure you that the next corpse to be found in Wickham Wood might well have been *yours*.'

'Do you mean to say that you have not enjoyed the liberties I have taken since our wedding night?'

'*That*,' she declared, with a very direct look, 'is another matter entirely.'

John laughed, but had to own that conduct befitting man and wife was very different from that permitted between unmarried persons. Having quizzed her enough, however, he reverted to their former topic of conversation.

'Upon reflection, I am inclined to think,' he said, 'that we should not be separated while questioning these people.'

She conceded that this was a much better plan, merely mentioning that it might present a problem where James Bromley was concerned.

'I only hope I may be able to persuade the authorities to permit me to speak with him.' He seemed somewhat doubtful.

'Of course you will!'

'I am glad you show such proper respect for my powers of persuasion.'

She gave him a very saucy look.

'You persuaded me to marry you, did you not?'

'There was never any question about that, was there?' he retorted.

So it was settled, and the rest of the walk was taken up with admiring the fine scenery and stealing a kiss or two behind a convenient hedge. After all, one could not allow foul murder to spoil one's enjoyment entirely.

4

The Unwelcome Guests

Supper, they were informed, was at seven o'clock in the evening, precisely. If they wished, however, they might join the others in the Gold Room before that time. With such encouragement, John and Lydia made their way towards this imposing chamber at half past six.

Moving along the hall, John was surprised for a moment when Lydia stood quite still and placed her forefinger over her lips in a time-honoured gesture. The door of the Gold Room was ajar and the voices of Fallowfield's residents carried clearly in the stillness.

'What is it, my dear?' John whispered.

'I wish,' she said, 'to hear something of what these people are thinking and saying when we are not by them.'

'Signora Machiavelli . . . ' he muttered wickedly.

'It may prove useful,' she countered, making a face at him.

'I cannot deny it.'

In truth, it was doubtful that the other members of the household would behave naturally in their presence, especially once they knew why they had remained here. While it might not be strictly within the bounds of propriety, eavesdropping could be a most beneficial tool in an enterprise such as this one.

' . . . seemed quite . . . respectable, in a somewhat common way.'

They could discern from the voice that the speaker was Mrs Leverett. An unknown masculine voice answered her.

'Don't see what business they have here,' it said gruffly.

'They are here at my invitation,' Portia replied, apparently quite unruffled by his disapprobation.

'Why you must foist a couple of Sussex mushrooms upon us, I cannot understand.'

'They are here to discover who shot Uncle Benedict.'

'We know very well who is responsible for your uncle's death,' the male voice barked back at her.

'I think not.'

'But I do not see how Mr and Mrs Savidge can help, my dear,' Mrs Leverett spoke again. 'They are very young. Indeed, the wife seems scarcely out of the schoolroom; and Mr Savidge did not strike me as precisely needle-witted.'

In the hallway, Lydia cast a speaking glance at John, barely managing to suppress a giggle.

'Mrs Savidge is but eighteen, but her husband is almost two and twenty.'

'Practically in his dotage, then!' the gentleman responded with exaggerated sarcasm.

'Mrs Wardle-Penfield speaks very highly of both of them.' This, from Portia, was uttered in tones which indicated that such a recommendation was not to be lightly dismissed.

'They may be quite unexceptionable.' Mrs Leverett's tone, however, conveyed that she remained unimpressed. 'I believe you said that Mr Savidge is the son of an innkeeper?'

'A very wealthy innkeeper,' Portia qualified. 'Why, the Savidges have just purchased Bellefleur, the estate of the late Sir Hector Mannington. It is quite as large, and even more ancient, than Fallowfield, Mama.'

'Is it indeed?'

'A sad end to an illustrious name,' the lone gentleman remarked, refusing to be placated by *nouveau-riche* pretensions.

'I have an idea,' John whispered to his wife.

'What is it?'

'A little play-acting.' He gave her a wink.

'What roles shall we play?'

'Let me deliver a soliloquy or two,' John said with a grin. 'Your task will be to observe the reactions of our audience.'

'Very well,' Lydia said, somewhat doubtfully. She would not criticize her husband, but privately doubted his abilities as a thespian.

Nonetheless, she took his arm and they made a dignified entrance into the drawing-room, which produced a moment of somewhat awkward silence. No doubt the room's occupants were wondering what, if anything, their guests had heard of their conversation.

★ ★ ★

To their surprise, there were four persons gathered in the Gold Room. Mrs Leverett and Miss Leverett, of course, were already known to them. The others were soon introduced: Mr Lawrence Chetwin, of whom Portia had already spoken to them, and Miss Delia Padgett.

Mr Chetwin was a large, hearty man with a martial bearing most appropriate in one who had been a cavalry officer before selling out of the army. Still, Lydia, who had been imagining him as a quiet man completely under the late Sir Benedict's thumb, now had to adjust her ideas considerably. Mr Chetwin had the air of someone accustomed to wielding authority. Not a young man — she would judge him to be rather past the age of fifty — he was very well-preserved with a fine figure, a full head of sandy-grey hair and a ruggedly attractive countenance.

Miss Padgett was a woman perhaps ten years Mr Chetwin's junior, and as shy and retiring as the gentleman was bluff and self-assured. She had been studiously silent while Lydia and John listened from the hallway, and remained so for most of the evening. She possessed the faded remains of a face once mildly pretty, along with the manner of someone all too accustomed to being snubbed or ignored. They soon learned that she had been Portia's governess, and had stayed on at Fallowfield as a sort of superannuated dependant and companion. It was a kinder fate than most of her profession could claim.

There was a flurry of subdued greetings, followed by a few moments of half-hearted attempts at conversation before Mr Chetwin addressed John.

'Your father is an innkeeper, I understand, sir?' he asked, not entirely able to disguise the contempt in his voice.

'He owns the Golden Cockerel, the finest inn in Diddlington,' John answered, quite unruffled.

'*My* father is a solicitor in Shepperton,' Lydia offered, forestalling any similar question.

'And is not your sister soon to marry Sir Reginald Pevensey?' This was from Portia. 'I believe my godmother mentioned as much in her most recent letter.'

'We shall be going up to London for the wedding in November,' Lydia agreed.

'It will be quite a romp, no doubt,' Mr Chetwin commented.

'It will be tolerably amusing.' Lydia chose to ignore his implication, but added wickedly, 'I am only sorry that my aunt, the Comtesse d'Almain, will be unable to attend.'

Mr Chetwin was temporarily silenced, as she had intended. Mrs Leverett, however, was instantly diverted.

'Your aunt is a member of the French nobility?' she asked, leaning forward in her eager curiosity.

'Through marriage.' Lydia nodded, and was assailed by questions relating to her relations, which only ceased when they went in to dinner several minutes later.

All proceeded uneventfully at first. The main course of their meal was a ragout of beef, excellently prepared, though accompanied by side dishes of somewhat inferior quality. It was the equal of anything served in the homes of most country gentlemen, however, and even Mrs Wardle-Penfield would not have found much to decry.

'Do you intend to remain here very long, Mr Savidge?' Mr Chetwin suddenly demanded of John.

'Really, Lawrence — ' Mrs Leverett protested, but was forestalled by John himself.

'No longer than is necessary to prevent what appears to be a serious miscarriage of justice.'

'Mis-carriage . . . of . . . justice,' Mr Chetwin repeated, each syllable sharply enunciated, as though sliced by a knife. 'Much do you know about it!'

'It is my understanding that the evidence against the young man is hardly compelling.' John adopted a tone of solemn censure, reminding Lydia of a more subdued version of his papa. 'The Scripture says that we should not judge, lest we be judged; and I believe that, under the Law of Moses, a man could not be convicted of a capital offence, except on the testimony of three witnesses.'

'We are Englishmen, sir, not Israelites!'

'But our religion is of the same lineage, sir.

As Christians, we are obliged to temper justice with mercy.'

'The man is no more than a common felon, and should be hanged,' Mr Chetwin cried, a flood of red rising up from his neck into his cheeks.

'I will not have you speak so of the man I love!' Portia shouted back at him, rising up from her chair and glowering across the table.

'Love!' This word only seemed to further enrage the gentleman. 'What do you know of love, miss? Running after a stable hand, acting like the veriest — '

'That is enough, Winny,' Mrs Leverett interrupted him. 'It is certainly not your place to condemn my daughter.'

'No, ma'am,' Mr Chetwin agreed. 'It is *your* place, and it is more the pity that you have forgotten it.'

Lydia carefully observed each of them. Portia and Winny were both in a towering rage, while Portia's mother merely seemed put out of countenance. Miss Padgett had the look of a dormouse cornered in the barn by a particularly hungry cat. If she swooned, it would be no surprise at all.

'You go too far, sir.'

'Sir Benedict would be alive today, were it not for James Bromley,' Mr Chetwin said, his tone less strident but equally confident. 'I am

43

as certain of that as I am of anything in this world.'

'But you are wrong,' Portia answered.

Mrs Leverett, however, could not let the matter rest there.

'It must have been James, dearest,' she told her daughter. 'After all, who else can possibly have done it?'

'Someone in this household,' John put in before anyone else could speak. 'Someone, perhaps, at this very table!'

★　★　★

The only person in the room who moved or spoke at this pronouncement was Miss Padgett. She gave a shriek of protest, pressing her handkerchief against her lips to stifle the sound. Everyone else was unnaturally stiff and silent until Miss Leverett herself spoke up.

'Most unlikely, I should think,' she said, but could not resist a speculative glance at her companions.

'It is too bad, sir!' Her mother's appearance of pained surprise was quite genuine for once, Lydia surmised. 'You come here as a guest in our house, and practically accuse us all of murder.'

'Not all of you,' John corrected quietly. 'In

all probability, it is only one of you.'

'By heaven, sir!' Mr Chetwin's wrath continued unabated. 'If I were younger, and my eyes had not failed me, I would call you out for this. So I would.'

'I hope that you would not be tempted to do anything so ill-advised, sir.' On these words, John rose from the table and motioned for Lydia to do likewise. 'My wife and I have been asked to remain here to right a wrong, and we intend to do so.'

'It is all nonsense . . . a waste of time.'

'Perhaps so, Mr Chetwin,' John said. 'Nevertheless, we have made a bargain and intend to keep it.'

Miss Leverett apparently deemed it time to bring this interesting discussion to an end. She stepped away from the table and turned to John.

'Perhaps I had better show you to Uncle Benedict's study.'

John and Lydia bade goodnight to the others and followed her out of the room. She walked very quickly, the rustle of her skirts like a sighing wind in the silent hallway. They had not gone very far before she stopped and flung open a door, indicating that they should pass through into the room beyond.

'You may examine the room as much as you like,' she told them. 'I cannot imagine what you expect to find.'

'Perhaps nothing.' John was quite unperturbed. 'But one never knows.'

'I shall be back directly.' She looked at him with patent disapproval, remarking, 'While I admire directness, Mr Savidge, there are times when a little restraint is called for.'

Without waiting for a response, she whirled about and left the room.

'We have ruffled a few feathers tonight, and no mistake,' John said to Lydia.

'But feather-ruffling is of all things my delight!'

His lips twitched. 'I thought it might be.'

'I cannot help wondering' — Lydia moved across to the large desk which dominated the room — 'what Mr Chetwin was about to call Miss Leverett before he was so rudely interrupted by her mama.'

'*Behaving like the veriest* ... ' John quoted, adding, 'Doxy, perhaps?'

'If I were to wager any amount upon the matter, I would put my money on *trollop*, although *light-skirt* has a certain ring to it, I confess.'

'But back to the matter at hand.'

John looked about him at the book-lined shelves before following Lydia to the desk. The top of the desk contained an ink-stand, quill pen, small lamp and a gilded snuff-box, all neatly arranged.

'Very tidy was Sir Benedict,' Lydia muttered.

'A military man.' John nodded assent. 'Not given to ostentatious display.'

He pulled open the top drawer on the right-hand side of the desk, where a few papers lay, perfectly stacked inside.

'Most convenient.'

'What is it?'

'A copy of the deceased's last will and testament.'

'Lying in plain view?' As the daughter of a solicitor, Lydia was scandalized. 'That is not the most sensible of places for it.'

'I would imagine' — John opened the drawer on the opposite side — 'that the legatees were all quite aware of what their inheritance would be.'

'Perhaps. But it still seems very odd to me.'

'You may have noticed, my dear, that this is a very odd sort of household in general.'

John examined the papers in the second drawer, then his brows drew together in a frown of concentration and he turned his attention to the first drawer once again. His gaze moved back and forth between the two, and it was clear to Lydia that something was amiss.

'What is wrong, John?'

'Do you discern any difference between these two?'

Lydia came around to stand over his shoulder, looking down at the desk and the two open drawers. At first glance they appeared identical, except for the contents. The second drawer appeared to hold a receipt book and a few slips of paper. Closer inspection, however, revealed something else.

'On the outside they are the same,' she said slowly. 'But the one on the right seems to be somewhat more shallow on the inside.'

'Precisely.'

'A false bottom!' she exclaimed.

'Not the most original idea, but reasonably efficient.' Her husband removed the documents in the top portion of the drawer and pried open the compartment beneath.

The contents were not immediately of a startling nature. It held two sheets of paper, folded but not sealed. Lydia, her head bent beside her husband's, perused its contents along with him, her eyes growing round with excited surprise.

'Well, well,' John said with his usual placidity. 'A most interesting discovery indeed.'

5

Where There's a Will

As they peered down at the papers, a faint rustle informed them that Miss Leverett had returned. She stood framed by the doorway, her gown of golden taffeta reflecting the lamplight, watching them intently.

'What have you there?' she asked.

'Your uncle's will,' Lydia answered.

'Oh yes.' Portia shrugged carelessly. 'He always kept it in the right-hand drawer of his desk. Everyone knew of it.'

John looked back at her, his face inscrutable. 'Did they also know that he had made another will, apparently on the night of his death?'

'Another will!' It was clear from her expression that this was a most unwelcome revelation to the young lady. 'That is absurd. Why would he do such a thing?'

'I would say,' Lydia remarked wryly, 'that his intention was essentially to disinherit *you*, Miss Leverett.'

'What!'

'His old will, which was on the top of the drawer, left the bulk of his estate to yourself.'

'Yes. I know. I am, after all, his nearest relation.'

'His new will, on the other hand, does not mention your name.'

'You mean that I will receive nothing — nothing at all!'

'You *would* have received nothing, if the will had been valid.'

'Is it not?'

'It does not bear your uncle's signature, nor that of any witness.'

'Thank heavens!'

'I think the old will must stand.'

'If he intended to disinherit me,' Portia asked, 'to whom did he leave the estate? To Mama?'

'See for yourself.'

John handed her the folded document, which she snatched from him and proceeded to read with some concentration. It was not difficult to tell when she reached the portion in question, for her mouth fell open in complete incredulity, not unmixed with anger.

'Winny!' she cried with supreme disgust.

'Exactly.'

★ ★ ★

For a moment, the trio in the study was silent. Each of them was wrestling with the startling new possibilities which this discovery had opened.

There seemed little doubt that Sir Benedict had been aware of his niece's affair with the stable hand. That he intended to punish her by his actions was almost certain. Whether he had meant to carry out such a threat, it was more difficult to establish. Had he merely been planning to use it to force her to put an end to her outrageous behaviour, or was he so thoroughly offended as to cast her off completely?

In either case, it was clear that Miss Portia Leverett had more than one reason to wish her uncle dead. Of course, she seemed genuinely surprised to learn of the existence of the will. But was she? On the other hand, if she *had* known of it, would it not have been more intelligent to dispose of it altogether? Presumably nobody would have been the wiser, and the former will would have been accepted without question. Or perhaps she had been unable to find it?

'I swear to you that I knew nothing of this,' the young lady said, pretty well judging the thoughts of the others.

'And James?' Lydia enquired.

'How could he possibly have known, if I did not?'

John drummed his fingers lightly upon the fine-grained wood of the desk. Lydia considered the girl before her and wondered to herself.

'It might be best,' John said at last, 'if you do not mention this to anyone just yet.'

'Very well.' Portia nodded her consent.

'And what of your uncle's pistols?'

'They are here,' she replied, going over to a plain wood cabinet, which was locked but with the key protruding from the lock so as to make it a useless accoutrement. She retrieved a small, flat box and brought it over to John.

Inside were the two guns, well kept and looking as though they had never been used. In spite of Lydia's ignorance of firearms, she could see that they were well made. John, rather more versed in such matters, pointed out the saw-handle style, the hair triggers and long barrels.

'Is there anyone at Fallowfield who can be termed a tolerable shot with these?' he enquired, handling one of the weapons gingerly.

Miss Leverett hesitated for a moment. 'Winny was considered a crack shot in his day,' she mused aloud. 'But his eyesight is so poor now that I doubt he could hit a stagecoach at ten paces.'

'Is no one else accustomed to handling

guns?' Lydia persisted.

'Uncle Benedict taught me how to shoot before I had left the schoolroom,' she confessed. 'With neither son nor nephew, he had to content himself to play mentor to his niece.'

Lydia and John exchanged a telling glance, but said nothing.

'I did not shoot my uncle, however,' the young lady ventured, as though resigned to playing the role of murderess.

'We never said that you did,' John reminded her.

'You did not need to do so.'

'I assure you, Miss Leverett,' he said, 'that I am not in the habit of leaping to conclusions without any evidence to support them.'

* * *

Deciding that they had done enough for one evening, John and Lydia prepared to retire to their bedchamber. Portia had already bade them goodnight, and they left the study to make their way upstairs.

Stepping out into the hallway ahead of John, Lydia was startled by a voice calling out from several feet away:

'Miss Padgett! . . . Delia!'

She turned around to find Mr Chetwin

advancing towards her. Since she was the only other person present in the hallway, John having lingered to straighten the papers in Sir Benedict's desk, Lydia correctly inferred that she had been mistaken for the older woman.

'I beg your pardon, sir,' she said quietly. 'Miss Padgett has already retired for the evening, I believe.'

In the subdued light, she could not be certain whether or not the gentleman blushed, but he was unquestionably disconcerted.

'Forgive me, ma'am,' he said, just as John emerged from the study. 'I was mistook.'

'Very understandable, I'm sure,' John assured him.

'Miss Padgett's gown and mine are almost identical in colour, and we are much alike in size.'

Mr Chetwin merely nodded at this, as if eager to dismiss the matter as quickly as possible. Clearly the dimness of his sight still irked him, though they were given to understand that it was an affliction from which he had suffered for several years. Sir Benedict had spared no expense in seeking remedies for his friend's condition, but nothing had availed.

'Well, goodnight to you both.'

They left him behind in the hall, and were

soon back at their own room.

'Poor man,' Lydia shook her head sadly. 'I wonder what he would have said had he known how near he came to being master of this house.'

'I wonder what you would say if you knew how near you are to being kissed!' her husband replied.

There followed a very pleasant interval, after which both John and Lydia fell into the sleep of sheer exhaustion. For Lydia it was a short-lived reprieve. She soon found herself dreaming that she was walking toward the Temple of the Seven Virtues. It was dark, but she could clearly discern two figures which dashed past her in the moonlight. The first was Portia Leverett, and the second was none other than Sir Benedict himself. She recognized him from the portrait which she had seen hanging in the study earlier that evening.

Suddenly there was the unmistakable sound of a gunshot. She ran to the temple. The door was wide open, and a figure was standing in the entrance. It was Sir Benedict, laughing lustily. On the floor beside him lay Portia's body, drenched in blood. Sir Benedict turned to Lydia and cried,

'She'll not be meeting James here any longer, I suppose!'

He winked at Lydia, entered the temple,

and slammed the door in her face.

Lydia sat upright in bed, sleep banished. Beside her, John stirred slightly and then settled back into slumber. Should she wake him? But to what purpose? A dream, however peculiar, was of no importance.

For a long time she sat there, thoughts weaving aimlessly in and out of her mind. Had Portia murdered her uncle? If so, would she confess in the end, rather than see her lover hanged? And what of Lawrence Chetwin? Was it possible that his blindness — well, not quite blindness, but near enough — could be feigned? Then there was Mrs Leverett. What if she had followed Sir Benedict to the temple and —

A slight sound in the hallway outside prompted her to get up and go to the door of her bedchamber. She opened it an inch or two and peered through the aperture just in time to see a female figure in a pale dressing-gown enter the room directly opposite theirs. Lydia imagined that her sister, Louisa, would have immediately swooned at this sight, assuming that she had seen a ghost. For herself, however, she was almost certain that it was Miss Padgett.

John's watch lay atop a chest beside the doorway. Picking it up and carrying it over to the window, Lydia was just able to discern that it was half-past two o'clock in the morning. Whatever was the mouse-like Miss Padgett doing, flitting about the house at such an hour?

Might she also, Lydia began to wonder, have been flitting about the grounds of Fallowfield on the night Sir Benedict was killed? It was an intriguing thought.

6

Which is the Man?

'You do not look at all the thing,' John said to his wife the following morning, with most unloverlike candour.

'I did not sleep very well,' she informed him.

'Poor honey.' He was all concern.

'But I observed something particularly interesting while you were lying in blissful oblivion.'

She related the unusual behaviour of the former governess, which caused him to raise his brows.

'What is one to make of that, I wonder?' he asked.

'In other circumstances, I would have suspected a secret tryst with a lover,' Lydia admitted.

'Ah!' John chuckled. 'But with whom could she possibly have such a rendezvous?'

'The butler, perhaps?' she suggested hopefully.

'Most improbable, I should think.'

Further speculation was suspended, however, by the call of duty. They both realized the morning was somewhat advanced and they had wasted precious time. After all, they had only three days to settle this matter. Last night they had made an interesting discovery, but this was no time to rest upon their laurels.

Going down together, they soon found that the other residents of the house had already breakfasted. The fact that their guests were so tardy would doubtless be another black mark against them. Even so, since they were both excessively hungry, they consumed a considerable amount of the food generously provided — which included eggs, ham, scones with strawberry jam, and several cups of coffee.

Just as they were finishing this repast, their patroness appeared, looking rather less confident than she had on the previous day. Her morning gown was rather more subdued than the ensemble displayed yesterday, being a pale lilac shade with a white lace collar.

'Are you going to be doing anything today?' she asked them, as though expecting them to spend the day sipping tea and exchanging gossip.

'I think we should establish a headquarters

of sorts,' John replied, taking a final sip of coffee. 'Your late uncle's study would seem to be the natural place to conduct our . . . interviews . . . with your family and the servants.'

'As you wish.' She continued to eye them with some speculation.

'We should, perhaps, begin with your mama, my dear,' Lydia said.

'Very well.'

'You may accompany her, if you wish.'

Portia gave a rather wry smile. 'Thank you. I do indeed wish it.'

★   ★   ★

While the Savidges made their way to the study, Portia went in search of her mother. Within ten minutes, the four of them were seated comfortably, with the door firmly closed to discourage any eavesdroppers.

Mrs Leverett remained in her exaggerated mourning attire, which should have been very solemn but continued to provoke Lydia with the urge to dissolve into inappropriate laughter.

'Ah!' the older woman said with a deep sigh. 'What memories are kindled by the familiar objects in this chamber. Poor, dear Benedict!'

'Well,' John said cheerfully, 'we had better get on with it, hadn't we?'

A frown marred the widow's tearful countenance, which was clearly visible, as she had lifted the dark veil and draped it over the crown of her head, making her look like an aged Madonna.

'I really do not know how I can be of any use to you,' she complained. 'I know nothing of this terrible business, I assure you.'

'We only wish you to tell us anything you may recollect about that day, ma'am. Sometimes even the most insignificant detail may be of more importance than one might imagine.'

Lydia tried to appear as solemn and as obsequious as possible. She must have managed tolerably well, for Mrs Leverett's rigid demeanour soon began to soften as she considered herself once more to be the centre of her audience's attention.

'If you think it will help, I will certainly do my best.' Here she closed her eyes for a moment, and pressed a delicate palm momentarily to her brow. 'Though it is almost more than I can bear to dwell on a day which will forever hang like a dark thundercloud over my heart and mind!'

'I daresay you can scarcely remember anything about that day,' her daughter said practically. 'It was, in all respects, a very ordinary one.'

'Ordinary!' Mrs Leverett could not accept this blithe description. 'I hope that you do not mean Mr and Mrs Savidge to believe that murder is an everyday occurrence at Fallowfield.'

'Forgive me,' Portia corrected herself. 'I only meant that the day seemed perfectly ordinary until my uncle was killed.'

This, as it turned out, was no more than the truth. Although Mrs Leverett did all in her power to squeeze every drop of melodrama from the situation, nothing in her narrative seemed at all remarkable. From the details of her morning toilette, to her altercation with a housemaid for opening the curtains in the drawing-room when she must have been quite aware that the sunlight would assuredly bring on a monstrous headache in her mistress, there was neither jot nor tittle which seemed to shed any light at all upon the matter.

'And did you hear the sound of the gun being fired, ma'am?'

'I'm afraid not,' Mrs Leverett admitted. 'I must have been fast asleep, and knew nothing until Portia's frantic cries alerted the household with the news of horror and doom. But then,' she added, descending to the mundane realm of strict fact, 'the temple is some distance from the house, and I am a very sound sleeper.'

'What happened when your daughter returned that night?' Lydia enquired, watching the older woman's face.

'There was a loud knocking at the door of my bedchamber, as Delia — Miss Padgett, that is — was shouting hysterically that Benedict was murdered.' She paused here, her face looking suddenly pinched in the effort of concentration. 'In truth, I thought she must have been having a nightmare. Then I heard Portia calling out, and Winny shouting in the background. He kept saying, 'You must be mistaken, girl! It cannot be Benedict. Surely not *Benedict*.'

'One could hardly blame him for doubting something so fantastic,' she mused. 'A man comes through war and pestilence unscathed, and then is murdered on his own grounds! What could be more fantastic than that?'

It seemed that the interview was about to conclude, when John asked one quite unexpected question:

'Were you aware, Mrs Leverett, that on the very evening of his death, Sir Benedict had made a new will, disinheriting Miss Leverett and leaving his entire estate to Mr Chetwin?'

Lydia was afraid that the widow was about

to swoon. She was completely silent, the colour draining from her face before rushing back with increased vigour. As she reddened alarmingly, so the power of speech returned to her, with calamitous results.

'What!' she almost shrieked in a comical combination of anger and surprise. 'I do not believe it!'

'It is true, Mama,' Portia informed her. 'I have seen the document myself.'

'How dare he!' Pamela Leverett's wrath overcame all restraint and any lingering sense of decorum which she might have possessed. 'How could he be so vile — so cruel — as to disinherit his own daughter!'

★ ★ ★

It was now the turn of the other three occupants of the room to be struck dumb. John's eyebrows rose almost into his hair and Lydia's eyes opened so wide that she wondered if her eyelids would ever appear again. Their reaction, however, was nothing to that of Mrs Leverett's only child. Portia's jaw dropped so swiftly and so low that it seemed her chin would come to rest on her bosom.

'What are you saying, Mama?' she ejaculated. 'Sir Benedict was my uncle, not my father!'

'Y-yes, of course, my dear.'

Mrs Leverett must have recollected herself, somewhat later than was convenient, and attempted to make some recompense for her lapse. Unfortunately, it was one of her less compelling performances, with a distinct lack of conviction.

'My father,' Portia repeated with deliberate slowness, 'was Uncle Benedict's brother, Harris, was he not?'

'Of course, my dear,' Mrs Leverett repeated mechanically, immediately spoiling this assertion by adding, 'At least, I am *almost certain* that Harris was your father.'

'Almost certain . . . ' Portia echoed, while Lydia struggled mightily to refrain from going into whoops.

'Well — ' Mrs Leverett fidgeted with the end of her veil, pressing her lips into a thin line. 'Really, they were both quite mad for me at the time. I was in two minds as to which of them to choose . . . '

'So,' Lydia prompted, 'in fact, either of the two brothers could well have been Miss Leverett's father?'

'No, no,' the mother protested, regaining her composure. 'I am absolutely certain that it was Harris.'

'And yet,' John reminded her, 'you stated quite otherwise only a few moments ago.'

'Oh, that!' She waved her hand, dismissing what she clearly considered to be a mere bagatelle. 'I do not say that I never suggested to Benedict that he *might be* your father, Portia. It was only a jest, of course, but . . . well . . . '

'Well, what?' It was clear that the younger girl was still trying to adjust her perceptions to this new, and most unwelcome, possibility.

'After all,' — Portia's mama drew herself up proudly, delivering her *apologia* — 'what harm was there in allowing him to believe that you were his daughter? Fallowfield was his to dispose of as he wished. There was no entailment, or anything of that kind involved, thank heaven! And he had no children to inherit. I know that, as his niece, you were likely to be chosen as his heiress, but this little . . . subterfuge . . . meant that it was almost unthinkable for him to do otherwise.'

'I am ashamed . . . appalled!' Portia was now every bit as dramatic as her mother, standing and orating majestically. 'Do you mean to say that you were cavorting with both brothers at the same time? With Papa and Uncle Benedict?'

'Or,' Lydia put in wickedly, 'with Papa and Uncle Harris, as the case may be.'

Neither lady paid any heed to this aside, and Portia continued her speech.

'And you kept this from me all these years!'

'A fine one you are to be ripping up at me about hiding things, miss!' the widow shot back, her tones losing a little of their refinement in the heat of the moment. 'The fact is, your own behaviour with that brute, James Bromley, has ruined all my schemes. I warned you that it was folly to become involved with someone of his class. It will be a miracle if we don't end up begging on the streets.'

John, who had been as mesmerized as anyone by her performance, here put an end to her lament by stating what no one had yet told the unfortunate woman.

'You are labouring under a misapprehension, Mrs Leverett,' he said. 'The will in question was never signed. I am reasonably certain that Miss Leverett remains her uncle's — er, her father's — heiress.'

For an instant, the woman was quite taken aback, then with equal suddenness her face was once more magically glowing with restored happiness.

'Then what on earth is all the fuss about?' She smiled sunnily upon them all. 'You gave me such a fright, Mr Savidge. It was very naughty of you not to tell me all at once.'

'Were you aware, madam, that your brother-in-law knew of your daughter's connection with the stable hand?'

'I am sure he did not,' Mrs Leverett answered confidently. 'He must have only just discovered it, or I do not doubt that he would have confided in me.'

'Unless he did not wish to alarm you, perhaps?' Lydia suggested.

'Perhaps.' The other woman seemed to turn the matter over in her mind. 'But he could not have kept his knowledge from me for very long.'

'We are much obliged to you for your . . . assistance, Mrs Leverett,' John said with a gentle dismissal.

Portia, however, was not yet finished.

'Yes, you are most helpful, Mama,' she said, glaring. 'You helped my uncle into your bed often enough, it seems!'

'There is no need to be crude, Portia.' Her mother lowered the veil over her face.

But Miss Leverett could not be mollified. She did not find it quite so easy to accept the fact that her father's identity was something of a mystery. In vain did her mother chide her about her own less than respectable liaison. Portia responded that at least she knew beyond question who was the father of her unborn child. This reference to her delicate

68

condition merely served to infuriate her mother, however, and it was some time before John and Lydia could calm them enough for them to leave the room without scratching at each other's eyes.

7

What the Gardener Heard

'Well,' Lydia remarked when the two women had quit the room, 'that was a most revealing conversation.' 'Indeed, one cannot miss the resemblance between mother and daughter.'

'They each seem to have a penchant for enjoying the pleasures of the flesh before their wedding day — though I would say that Mrs Leverett looked to rise socially by her connections, while her daughter is less mercenary.'

'Or less sensible.' John shrugged. 'But this does not help us a great deal in our enquiries.'

Lydia agreed. Had Mrs Leverett known of the change in her brother-in-law's will, it might have opened up a new avenue for them to pursue. However, her surprise and chagrin were undoubtedly genuine. She was not so good an actress that she could have feigned such emotions convincingly. Nor was she likely to have betrayed herself so completely before her daughter, except in a moment of shock and anger. It was unlikely that she had murdered the poor man to ensure that the will was never signed and that her daughter would inherit the estate. In short, it was not a promising beginning at all.

'I need some air.' Lydia went over to the window, unhooked the latch and threw it open, taking a deep breath.

She had hardly done so, however, when John's ears were assaulted by something between a gasp and a screech, which clearly betokened that his wife had been unpleasantly surprised.

'What is it, my dear?' he asked, both curious and concerned.

'I did not see you there, sir,' she said, ignoring him and directing her remark to someone outside the window.

'Sorry, miss,' a masculine voice answered. 'I was kneeling down behind the hedge, doing a bit of weeding, like. Didn't mean to scare you.'

Coming up behind her, John looked out above her head to see an elderly man with a thatch of thinning silver hair, standing less than ten feet away from them, with his hat held respectfully in his hand. He was visible only from the waist up, his lower portion being obscured by a neatly trimmed hedge. Between the hedge and the house was a narrow gravel path, and a few shrubs directly beneath the windows. Aside from that there was no obstruction.

'Are your thoughts the same as mine?' Lydia turned her head and looked up into her husband's face.

He said nothing, merely nodding and giving his faintly mischievous smile.

'Would you tell me, Mr . . . '

'Ormsby, sir,' the man replied.

'Mr Ormsby,' John continued, 'have you been weeding in this spot for many minutes?'

'More'n a quarter of an hour, sir,' Mr Orsmby said.

'And did you hear anything of what we were saying in this room?'

Mr Ormsby grew as red as a ripe cherry, dropping his gaze to the ground, but insisted that he didn't hold with listening to other people's private conversations.

'Of course not!' Lydia was quick to assure him that they were not accusing him of such unchristian behaviour. 'But sometimes one cannot help overhearing things when one is so close by.'

'True enough, ma'am.' But he reminded them that, in this instance, the window had been shut until Lydia herself opened it. Practically speaking, he was not likely to have heard much.

'Would you be so kind as to join us inside, Mr Ormsby?' John asked. 'We shall not keep you long.'

It was an invitation not to be lightly refused, and it was only a few minutes before the three of them were alone in the study. Lydia took the precaution of closing the window again, just in case there might be other gardeners lurking about.

★ ★ ★

'Now, sir,' John asked, being careful not to intimidate someone who might prove very useful to them, 'you are clearly someone of importance at Fallowfield, if you do not mind me saying so.'

The older man threw out his chest with some pride, declaring that he had been head gardener on the estate for near about twenty years, and in service here for almost forty years.

'I am not interested in what you may have chanced to hear today, Mr Ormsby,' John said gently. 'That is of no importance, believe me.'

'Just so, sir.'

'Can you tell me, then, if it was your

master's habit to leave the windows of his study open upon occasion.'

'He kept them open most times, sir,' the other man said positively. ''Cept at night, of course.'

'Of course.' John nodded in agreement, then added, 'And did you happen to be working near one of the study windows on the day that Sir Benedict was shot?'

'I was indeed, sir.'

'I do not suppose . . . ' — John proceeded somewhat warily here — 'that you overheard anything memorable that day?'

'Yes sir, I did!'

'You did?' Lydia could not refrain from echoing his words. It seemed incredible that they should have such good fortune.

'What was it that you heard, Ormsby?' John's eyes narrowed as he kept them fixed upon the man before him, not acknowledging his wife's small outburst.

'I was out by the hedge, sir, same as today,' he said unnecessarily. 'It must've been 'bout three o'clock or so when I heard a regular battle royal comin' from this room.'

'It was the master and Mr Kempton, goin' at it 'ammer and tongs.'

'Mr Kempton?' John frowned at the introduction of this mysterious personage.

'Sir Benedict's solicitor, that is,' Mr

Ormsby explained.

'They were arguing about something?'

The gardener confirmed that they were having a right set-to. He couldn't, he added apologetically, hear everything that was being said, but it must have been something to do with financial matters. The words of the two combatants carried fitfully through the open window, as their mutual ire rose and fell along with their voices.

' 'I've pulled you out o' the River Tick one too many times, Cuthbert', the Master said to Mr Kempton. Then Mr Kempton says, 'It ain't so much blunt this time, sir. I promise it's the last time'. But Sir Benedict wasn't 'aving any. He shouts back, 'By God, if I find you've been dippin' into money from the estate, you'll be wearin' a rope collar before very long!'

'After that,' Mr Ormsby concluded his tale, 'I didn't hear much more. It must've been just a minute before I heard the study door slam to, and my friend, Jack, saw Mr Kempton gallopin' away on his horse not more than five minutes later.'

When he had finished speaking, John and Lydia digested what they had just heard in silence. This was a most interesting development indeed.

'Are you absolutely certain,' John asked

presently, 'that this incident was the after-noon of the day that Sir Benedict was murdered?'

'Yes sir.'

'You have been very helpful.' John rose from behind the desk, and Mr Ormsby followed.

'I ain't goin' to get into trouble for this, sir?' The gardener eyed him with some misgiving. 'I couldn't help what I heard.'

'You are in no danger of persecution, sir.'

'Indeed, we are very grateful to you.' Lydia smiled encouragingly at him.

He went out, cap in hand, looking much relieved.

★   ★   ★

'An altercation with his solicitor on the very day of his death,' Lydia said slowly as the door closed behind him. 'A curious coincidence?'

'Or a motive for murder?' John finished her thought.

'Supposing Mr Kempton *had* been . . . borrowing . . . money from the estate?'

'If he had creditors dunning him for money, it is entirely possible.'

'I wonder why he should be in any financial difficulty?'

'That remains to be seen. But whatever the cause, it seems we must pay a visit to the Kemptons as soon as possible.'

'In the meantime,' Lydia said cheerfully, 'who shall be our next victim?'

'I think we should speak with Miss Padgett.'

'An excellent idea,' Lydia agreed. 'The poor thing is so timid that her nerves are likely to bring on the vapours if she is left waiting too long.'

Before this could be accomplished, they summoned their patroness to inform her of what they had just learned. Portia was still very much preoccupied with thoughts of her mother's recent revelation. She barely had patience enough to allow the others to explain what had transpired, so busy was she in deploring her mother's character and the fact that she had been quite ignorant of it for so long.

'I really do not know how I could have been so blind,' she cried, shaking her head in self-reproach. 'No wonder Sir Benedict was so interested in my future . . . and so annoyingly officious.'

'But you must let us tell you what we have just learned, my dear Miss Leverett,' Lydia at last managed to interject.

They related the gist of what Mr Ormsby

had told them, which distracted the young lady from her other dilemma. In fact, she was so pleased that she at once restored them to her good graces, saying that she now was certain that she had not wasted her time by persuading them to remain and look into this wretched business.

'Mr Kempton . . . ' She lingered upon the name, smiling sweetly. 'Of course he must have stolen back here and shot Uncle Benedict.'

'He could have surreptitiously removed the pistol during their argument, I suppose,' Lydia added, eager to encourage her in this more positive direction.

'We must apprehend him at once!'

'That we cannot do,' John said, squashing her enthusiasm.

'Why not?' she demanded, quite put out by his treachery.

'At the moment this is all supposition, my dear. We need more compelling evidence than this, if we are to persuade the authorities to release your James.'

In spite of her disappointment, Portia was practical enough to know that he was right.

'We are planning to go to Mr Kempton's home this evening,' Lydia told her, 'to see what else we can discover. Perhaps you could direct us there?'

'Direct you?' This was clearly not good enough for the vengeful miss. 'I shall accompany you myself. If Kempton is to be brought to justice, I wish to be there to see it.'

John rubbed his chin, giving the two women a considering glance.

'In the meantime,' he said, 'would you be so good as to instruct Miss Padgett to join us here?'

'Delia?' Portia was clearly surprised. 'I do not know what possible use she can be to us. I can assure you that she is quite incapable of killing anyone — even Uncle Benedict.'

'That may be so.' John smiled at her last words. 'But, like Mr Ormsby, she might have heard or seen something which could be of importance.'

This had obviously not occurred to Miss Leverett, but she immediately saw the sense in it. 'You are very clever, sir.' Her glance was admiring, her estimation of him rising with every minute. 'I should have known that my godmother would not regard you so highly if you were as foolish as you look.'

'Thank you,' he replied solemnly, while Lydia bit her lips and tried to keep a straight face. The inhabitants of Fallowfield were a source of almost ceaseless amusement. One never knew what they would say next.

Miss Leverett was just about to quit the

room when the door was flung open without ceremony and a large figure all but obscured the view without.

'There you are, my little bird!' a commanding voice boomed out. 'Have you been hiding from me, puss?'

8

The Giant and the Governess

'Sir Caleb,' Portia greeted the stranger, her tone and look indicating anything but pleasure at his unexpected arrival. 'What are you doing here, sir?'

'Is that any way to greet your most ardent admirer, miss?' he demanded rhetorically. 'I came to see how you were getting on since this sad tragedy. They told me you were here in the study.'

While Miss Leverett performed the necessary introductions, Lydia took the time to examine Sir Caleb Hovington. He was a man of about fifty, with a ruddy countenance and a manner which reminded her of John's papa — though clearly this gentleman was of the gentry. He was excessively rotund, his girth so ample that his striped waistcoat struggled to contain it. His manner with the young lady was that of a gentleman in determined pursuit of his quarry. Knowing what she did, Lydia considered his chances to be negligible.

On the other hand, if her precious James kept his appointment with the hangman, Miss Leverett might well deem a union with the unappealing Sir Caleb preferable to social disgrace. Personally, despite the fact that she was no longer as pleased with Miss Portia as she had first been, this made Lydia all the more determined to save the stable hand. To be married to something like Sir Caleb was a fate which few women were base enough to deserve.

'So you're here to save James Bromley's neck, eh?' Sir Caleb looked John over condescendingly. He cast a brief glance at Lydia, apparently dismissing her as unworthy of his notice. 'Wasting your time, sir. The man's as guilty as Judas, in spite of what Miss Leverett here may tell you. She is so sweet, my dear Portia, that she cannot think ill of anyone.'

For a moment Lydia toyed with the idea that Sir Caleb himself might have killed Portia's uncle. But she could think of no motive as yet. Besides which, she was inclined to doubt that he could have done the deed without being seen. Even on a dark night, he must have stood out like a white elephant in a dressing room. When one considered that he also appeared to be terribly buffle-headed, she felt it would be useless to consider something so unlikely.

'Oh, I am perfectly able to think ill of many people,' Portia attempted to disabuse him of his romantic illusions.

'I will not believe it,' he declared truthfully. Then, turning to John, he immediately rhapsodized: 'Tell me, is she not the fairest flower that ever bloomed in Hertfordshire?'

'If you will excuse us, sir, we must be continuing with our enquiries.' John ignored his comment and moved towards the door.

'Let God judge the matter, Mr Savidge,' Sir Caleb abjured him. 'Do not be forcing the hand of Providence.'

'I do not believe in God,' Portia announced, whether from genuine conviction or a desire to provoke her large suitor, Lydia could not be quite sure.

'Hush, my dear!' the gentleman cried, frowning. 'You should not say such things, even in jest.'

Portia was not impressed. 'You notice that I have not been struck dead by a lightning bolt, however.'

'I have often thought that atheism must be a very comfortable belief,' Lydia spoke her thoughts aloud.

'How so?'

'Well, in the absence of a divine lawgiver,' Lydia said, 'it must follow that man can make whatever laws he chooses without fear of any retribution.'

'Which would result in not only moral but social anarchy,' John remarked.

'Nonsense!' Portia dismissed this argument. 'Atheists may be just as moral and upright as anybody. They obey the Laws of Nature.'

'Which are morally ambiguous at best.'

'The cat eats the rat, the dog eats the cat,' Lydia offered as example, 'and the men of science nail the dog, alive and howling, to a board in order to vivisect it.'

'After all,' John continued, 'there is no logical reason for there to be a prohibition against killing one's mother-in-law, for example. Such rules are mere arbitrary restrictions based on foolish sentiment.'

'I know more than one woman who would gladly stick a dagger into their mother-in-law.' Lydia nodded sagely.

'Atheists may choose to follow the codes of traditional morality.' John eyed Portia with some amusement. 'But they do so on emotional rather than rational grounds.'

'Rules such as 'thou shalt not kill' are designed to preserve human society,' Portia argued, warming to her theme.

'But why should anyone wish to preserve society? Why should one sacrifice individual pleasure for the good of the wretched multitude?'

'And, if it comes to that,' Lydia pushed the argument further, 'why should a man not be allowed to rob his neighbour of house, land, or even wife, if those are what he desires?'

'Indeed, might not the murder of one's mother-in-law be considered an act of pure philanthropy?' John asked, returning to his previous example with perhaps too much relish. 'It might be argued, after all, that mothers-in-law are pernicious pests — perhaps not even human.'

'Really,' Lydia could not resist capping his argument, 'a society which prevents one from killing one's mother-in-law can hardly be considered civilized, can it?'

'You are all talking nonsense,' Sir Caleb interrupted their imaginings. 'Right and wrong will always be right and wrong, whatever else may change.'

'Do you think so?' John begged leave to disagree. 'Once one dispenses with a power outside of ourselves, anything and everything becomes permissible.'

'But we have strayed very far from our original intention,' Lydia reminded them all.

'Our intention was to uncover the truth,' her husband emphasized.

'But a particular truth — the innocence of

Mr Bromley — rather than a general one.'

'*Touché!*'

'Come, let us go into the drawing-room, sir.' Portia led Sir Caleb gently but firmly out into the hall, flinging over her shoulder, 'I shall send Miss Padgett to you directly.'

★   ★   ★

She was as good as her word, and it was not many minutes before a head appeared, peering around the edge of the door, a pair of anxious eyes surveying John and Lydia as the lady in question hesitated to enter.

'Good afternoon, Miss Padgett,' John said quietly.

'Do come in, ma'am,' Lydia added, with a welcoming and (she hoped) reassuring smile.

'I — I do not know what you can possibly want with me,' Miss Padgett muttered, slowly forcing herself to move forward until she reached the chair to which John motioned her.

'We are desirous of learning precisely what you can remember from the day that Sir Benedict was shot.'

'That is something I would prefer to forget, Mr Savidge,' the woman before them said, closing her eyes as if to blot out any stray image which might flit across her mind.

'Where were you at the time of Sir Benedict's death?' John persisted, watching her over the tips of his fingers which he leaned together before him like a high-pitched roof top.

She looked like a hunted animal, her eyes darting about, her hands fluttering in front of her like butterflies. If one were to judge purely by appearances, she betrayed every sign of guilt.

'Wh-where was I?' She was breathing heavily. 'Where was I?'

'Yes. Where were you?' John repeated patiently.

'I was in my bed, of course,' she gnawed at her lips. 'Where else should I be at such an hour?'

'Did you like Sir Benedict?'

'Did I like Sir Benedict?' Clearly she was in the habit of repeating everything, giving herself some time to consider the question before venturing upon an answer. 'He . . . he was not the sort of man . . . that is, very few people . . . I was not especially close . . . '

'I understand,' Lydia supplied helpfully, 'that the gentleman's character was perhaps somewhat autocratic?'

'Oh yes!' Delia Padgett almost gasped out the words in her relief at having someone else speak her thoughts so aptly. 'Not that he was cruel, you understand. I'm sure he was very generous to me, and . . . but there was no denying that he was quite overpowering at times.'

'So you did *not* like him?'

'No, no. I would never say such a thing!' she hastened to correct him. 'In truth, I had few dealings with him.'

As few as possible, Lydia surmised silently.

'And you recall nothing unusual about that day, Miss Padgett?'

'Nothing,' she answered, her first definite response yet.

'You say that you were in your bedchamber,' Lydia repeated her former statement. 'You generally retire early in the evening?'

'At half-past ten, or perhaps eleven o'clock,' the governess answered, gradually growing less agitated.

'Last night I could not sleep.' Lydia watched the other woman intently to see her reaction to what she was about to say. 'I happened to see you returning to your bedchamber at a very curious hour of the night — or rather, morning.'

The effect of this pronouncement was certainly startling. She had as well dashed a bucket of cold water over the poor unsuspecting woman.

'Whatever are you saying, ma'am?' Miss

Padgett rose from her chair, wringing her hands and looking wildly about her as one seeking an avenue of escape. 'I have never been accused of . . . and really, it is very hard to know that one is being spied upon . . . and I assure you that nothing in the least improper has ever passed between Mr Chetwin and myself . . . and you have no right, Mrs Savidge . . . '

'Pray compose yourself, Miss Padgett,' John urged, putting an end to her muddled speech.

Meanwhile, he treated Lydia to a look which she had no difficulty in interpreting. Neither of them had really considered that the poor little governess might be carrying on a clandestine affair with Mr Chetwin. Now, of course, they could hardly doubt that this was the case. As fantastic as it might seem, the mouse had managed to acquire a lover. He might not be young and handsome, but he was certainly more than a mere friend.

'I did not mean to imply that you were visiting any gentleman.' Lydia gazed at her in some astonishment. 'I merely wondered if you were in the habit of wandering about the house at odd hours, and whether you might have done so last week, on the night which we have been discussing.'

'I am not a strumpet, whatever you might choose to think!' The pathetic creature seemed not to hear what was being said, her eyes brimming with tears and actually on the point of hysteria. 'A woman in my position cannot . . . I have always tried to do what is right, but — '

'We are not here to reproach you, dear woman,' John said. 'We are only seeking the truth in the matter of murder.'

'I swear to you that I had nothing to do with it!' Miss Padgett cried in tones of anguish. 'Though I may be a fallen woman, I am no murderess. By all that is holy and true, I swear it!'

She promptly succumbed to a severe attack of the vapours, and it took some time for them to restore her to a measure of rationality. It was clear that there was small chance of acquiring any coherent information from her, so they soon released her, promising to say nothing of what she had revealed to them.

★   ★   ★

'Say what you like, but there is no shortage of revelations to be had here at Fallowfield,' John said, as soon as she was gone.

'But they are all of a personal nature, and irrelevant to the matter at hand,' Lydia complained.

'Not necessarily. After all, they reveal something of life here, and of the character of those who reside in this house. That may be the key to this mystery — if mystery it is.'

'You think it possible that Miss Leverett may be wrong, and that James Bromley is guilty?'

'Anything is possible.'

'After what we just learned from Miss Padgett, I should say so!' Lydia shook her head, even now hardly able to credit the truth. 'She is so staid, so quiet, so apparently respectable. One can hardly conceive of her being anyone's mistress.'

'Consider the circumstances, though.'

'How do you mean?'

'Mr Chetwin is all but blind, and confined to the house and its immediate environs. He had small choice in mistresses, I would imagine.'

'Yes,' she conceded. 'It seems that Miss Padgett was suffered to remain here as his nurse and companion.'

'She no doubt considered it a blessing, seeing that most governesses are cast off as soon as their charges are of age. Their fate is often an unhappy one of penury and loneliness.'

'One might well prefer to offer oneself to a man in exchange for some measure of security and comfort. It is an arrangement to their mutual benefit.'

'Precisely.' John nodded. 'We should not judge her too harshly.'

'I think we could not judge her more harshly than she does herself, poor woman.'

At this juncture, they were interrupted by Portia. She had finally got rid of Sir Caleb and had seen a weeping Miss Padgett fleeing up the stairs, presumably to the sanctuary of her bedchamber. Neither John nor Lydia felt it necessary to inform Portia of what they had just learned, merely saying that Miss Padgett's nerves could not endure the strain of recalling the tragic events surrounding Sir Benedict's demise.

'Poor, dear Delia,' Portia said, with a kind of fond contempt. 'She is the kindest-hearted woman in the world, but painfully shy and afraid of her own shadow. I do not know how she manages with Winny, but they seem to rub along tolerably well. He deals more gently with her than he does with most people.'

'She is of great use to him, no doubt.'

'Very much so.' Portia smiled. 'She is his guide around the walks at Fallowfield, she lays out his clothes for him, and reads to him each day. In addition, she listens attentively to all his old stories of military life which are a great bore for the rest of us.'

She had no idea, of course, that Miss Padgett provided other services for the gentleman. But all agreed that she was invaluable to one in his position.

'I think we should have Mr Chetwin come in next,' John said at last. 'Later this afternoon, I would like to try if I can meet with James Bromley, while Lydia accompanies you, Miss Leverett, to pay a call upon Mr and Mrs Kempton.'

'Before you proceed any further,' Portia said, 'there is something I wish to show you both.'

9

The Artist and the Old Soldier

She slipped from the room and was gone for only a few minutes, leaving the others both bewildered and undeniably intrigued. When she returned at last, she carried a sheaf of papers which she handled with great care. They were too large to be letters, or anything of that nature, and Lydia guessed that they were drawings of some kind. Perhaps Miss Leverett painted watercolours, though why she should wish to display them at this moment was incomprehensible.

'Look at this!' she cried triumphantly, spreading the papers out on the desk.

Lydia and John stared down at the work before them, and Lydia could not refrain from exclaiming, 'But these are very good, very good indeed.'

'I think them equal to anything by Stubbs. Do not you?'

John examined the work, which consisted of pencilled sketches of animals, most of them horses. Each curve and sinew was captured with such detail and such vivid power that one almost expected them to leap from the page.

'Quite remarkable,' John admitted.

'James drew them,' she said, at which both Lydia and John looked up in surprise.

'He has had only a few lessons with a local drawing master,' Portia explained. 'But his gift is far beyond ordinary talent. Do you not agree?'

'I think you are right,' Lydia said.

'And you, sir?' Portia asked a little anxiously.

'I am no expert in art, but I pride myself on my knowledge of horses, and these are some of the finest portrayals I have ever seen.'

'With a little encouragement, James can be a truly great artist. I am determined on it.'

Lydia felt that anything this young lady set her mind to, she was almost certain to accomplish. Portia admitted that she had first taken an interest in the young stable hand when she had seen one of the maids with a sketch which she recognized at once as a superior drawing to anything she had ever seen before. On learning that it was the work of someone on the estate, she had immediately sought him out. At first interested only in his abilities with a pencil, she could not deny that the young man's handsome face and sensitive nature had equal claim to her attention. A mutual passion for art had quickly led to a mutual passion for each other, with the inevitable result.

'I wanted you to see these before you meet James,' she said. 'He is no mere servant, Mr Savidge. Someday the whole of England — perhaps the whole world — will know the name of James Bromley.'

'That may be,' John acknowledged quietly. 'At the moment, however, I am merely anxious that *I* should get to know the young man before the end of the day, and discover whether he may have something to tell me which can help to save him from the gallows. Otherwise, he will be known to posterity merely as the murderer of an English country gentleman.'

This practical attitude brought Portia's flight of fancy down to earth with a thump. She could not, however, deny that common sense was more to the purpose at this point than artistic merit.

'I will see if I can find Winny, and whether we can persuade him to speak to you.'

★　★　★

Apparently Mr Chetwin was more easily persuaded than she had imagined, for not many minutes passed before he was at the study door. Unlike the lady before him, he did not hesitate. He crossed the threshold boldly and made his way to a chair, moving with such confidence that one could easily forget his impairment.

'You came alone, sir?' Lydia asked, having expected someone to escort him.

'I know every inch of this house and grounds, ma'am,' Lawrence Chetwin informed her with some pride.

'You really do not need Miss Padgett's assistance, then?' she asked, deliberately provocative.

He stiffened, but held his tongue, merely saying, 'Miss Padgett is of great use to me. At the moment she is reading to me from *Tristram Shandy*. Most amusing.'

'It is a blessing, then, that your hearing is still good.'

'My hearing, ma'am, is excellent.'

'I believe,' John said, 'that when one sense is diminished, another generally becomes more acute to compensate for its loss.'

'That is so.'

'Now, sir, if you would be so kind as to tell us about the day that Sir Benedict died.'

'This is all so much nonsense, if you ask me!' The older man continued in his opposition to their inquiry.

'Nevertheless, we have promised Miss Leverett to do what we can for her.'

'Precious little that is like to be.' Mr Chetwin snorted his contempt. 'A pair of children chasing wild geese!'

'Still, here we are,' Lydia said. 'And I hope that you will indulge us just a little, sir.'

He grunted, but relented enough to begin relating what he could remember of the fateful day, in rather excessive detail, perhaps. He had awakened at seven o'clock in the morning, precisely, as was his custom. His breakfast was paltry, consisting of one boiled egg and a slice of toast with coffee — black. After breakfast he went for a walk by the lake with Miss Padgett, then joined Sir Benedict in his study for a chat.

'What did you speak of, Mr Chetwin?' John asked.

'Oh, this and that,' he said rather evasively. 'He often asked my advice on estate matters, you know. I loved him like a brother, I tell you. Saved his life when we were lads.'

'So I have been informed.'

'His father took me in and treated me as one of the family,' he continued reminiscing. 'Ben and I even joined the army together. Ben bought me a commission too. That was back in '80. We were young blades then. What was it? Twenty — no, more than thirty

— years ago! Went to America, the two of us, and were there when Cornwallis surrendered at Yorktown. Dark days. Dark days.'

'Yes indeed.' Now John put an end to pointless sentiment by throwing in the question which had so enraged Mrs Leverett such a short while ago. 'Did you know, Mr Chetwin, that on the evening of his death, Sir Benedict made a new will which named you as his sole heir?'

Those faded eyes narrowed, as if trying to penetrate through the darkness to see whether he were being quizzed or not.

'I don't believe it!' he said at last, and Lydia could see that he was moved to tears by this news. 'Not but what it's the sort of thing he *would* do, especially seeing how his own flesh and blood was behaving!'

'Were you aware that he knew about Miss Leverett's affair with James Bromley?'

'No, I wasn't,' Chetwin answered flatly. 'But then, I had only just learned of it myself.'

'You never mentioned it to him?'

'Certainly not!' He drew himself up in his best military fashion. 'It was not my place to go telling tales which would likely break his heart, poor Ben. I knew he would find out in time.'

'He would not have concealed his knowledge, you think?'

'No, he would not.' He was quite definite on this point. 'Not from me, at least.'

'But it appears that he must have discovered the truth, since everything indicates that he went to the temple that night in order to confront his niece and her lover.'

'He must have found out about it that day,' Mr Chetwin agreed.

'Did you notice anything different about his demeanour that day?'

'Now that I think on it, he was looking rather blue-devilled that evening at supper.' He frowned, remembering. 'I didn't take much notice of it at the time, but he didn't have very much to say at table, and took himself off to his study as soon as we had all finished eating.'

'In order to make his new will, no doubt.'

'Am I to inherit Fallowfield, then?' Mr Chetwin asked bluntly.

'I'm afraid not, sir.' Lydia, watching her husband, was amazed at his inscrutable countenance as he related the fact that the will had been neither signed nor witnessed.

'He was going to threaten Portia with disinheriting her.' Mr Chetwin was speaking more to himself than to them. 'That's why he went to the temple, depend upon it.'

'You are probably right.'

'I tell you again, sir, if it wasn't for James

Bromley, Sir Benedict would be alive and well today.' His wrath began to boil once more, and he pounded his fist upon the desk before him in his rage. 'Let the man hang, I tell you! That's all his kind is good for.'

John ignored his outburst, continuing his questions. 'You say you have excellent hearing. Yet you did not hear the shot which killed Sir Benedict?'

'Of course I heard it,' Mr Chetwin snapped.

'Yet you did nothing about it?'

'I didn't know my best friend had been murdered, did I?' he said bitterly. 'I thought it was some drunken fool on the high road nearby, or a poacher in the woods. Why should I waken the household for that?'

It was a reasonable enough explanation, and it seemed that the interview was at an end. John was not quite done yet, however.

'Tell me, Mr Chetwin,' he asked, 'do you think that Sir Benedict would have left his estate to you if he had known of your own liaison with Miss Padgett?'

10

No Easy Task

For a moment, Lydia thought that John might be the next murder victim at Fallowfield. Mr Chetwin's face grew so dark, and the veins in his neck bulged out to such a degree, that she thought he was like to explode from his seat like a cannon ball and launch himself at her husband. His hands were white from gripping the arms of his chair, and he managed to control his temper enough to desist from physical assault. His tongue, however, he could not entirely restrain.

'You damned little innkeeper!' Somewhat to her surprise, he did not shout. Instead, his voice issued from between teeth so tightly clenched that his mouth seemed scarcely to move. 'How dare you speak of her in such a fashion!'

John was quite unmoved. 'You deny, then, that you are — um — romantically involved with Miss Padgett?'

'You, sir, are no gentleman.'

This, the supreme insult, had no visible effect upon Mr Savidge.

'No, sir, I am not. I am the son of an innkeeper, as you so kindly pointed out.'

'Miss Padgett is a good, kind lady. She does not merit your insults.'

'I do not believe,' Lydia interjected, 'that my husband has insulted her. He has merely asked you a question which you have not answered.'

'Shame on you, ma'am.' Mr Chetwin turned to face her. 'To be speaking of such things without so much as a blush — and you scarcely out of the schoolroom!'

'After what I have learned today, sir, it is a good thing that I am not missish, else I should have taken to my bed in a fit of strong hysterics.'

'I ask you again, sir.' John would not be deterred. 'If Sir Benedict disapproved so strongly of his niece's behaviour, would he not also have objected to yours?'

'*That*,' he asserted, 'was an entirely different matter.'

'I appreciate that the cases are not identical, and yet I cannot help but ask myself whether Miss Padgett would not have been summarily dismissed had her master known where and in what manner she was spending her nights.'

Mr Chetwin's lip curled into something

which bore a faint resemblance to a smile, but devoid of humour.

'Sir Benedict,' he said slowly, 'was hardly in a position to judge me, seeing that he was not averse to female companionship himself.'

'What do you mean, sir?' John frowned.

'My dear Mr Savidge, the delightful Pamela has been keeping his bed warm these fifteen years or more.'

'Pamela!' Lydia could not refrain from exclaiming unguardedly. 'Mrs Leverett?'

'The very same.'

★   ★   ★

Why Lydia should have been surprised at this, she did not know. At this point in their proceedings, she would have thought that nothing could ever shock her again. Still, she had to own that it was quite unexpected.

'Sir Benedict's sister-in-law was also his mistress?' John demanded, and Lydia could tell that he was almost as taken aback as herself.

'It was not entirely a novel situation for her,' Mr Chetwin remarked drily.

'I understand that both Sir Benedict and his brother had courted Mrs Leverett in their youth?'

'Courted!' The other man actually chuckled at this. 'It would be more accurate to say that she had seduced them both.'

Mr Chetwin proceeded to relate the details of the somewhat convoluted relations between Pamela Leverett, Sir Benedict Stanbury and his brother, Harris. Pamela — Miss Honeydale, as she was then — had been the most sought-after young lady in the country. Though her father was no more than a shopkeeper in Ware, she was undoubtedly a beauty, with an instinctive knowledge of how to captivate men.

It could not be denied that Benedict and Harris had both been hot for her. Benedict's intentions, however, were not precisely honourable. Having at last achieved his purpose, he continued to enjoy the young woman's company, unaware that his young brother had also succumbed to her not inconsiderable charms. When Miss Honeydale found herself in what is usually termed a 'delicate condition', she appealed to both men. The elder brother scorned her pleas, but the younger was *gudgeon enough* (Mr Chetwin's phrase) to insist upon doing right by her. He married her and accepted the daughter which she bore him as his own.

The happy couple moved to a nearby village, and Harris, at his brother's suggestion, adopted his mother's maiden name of Leverett. For almost five years they lived a life of quiet seclusion and apparent harmony, until Harris contracted a fever which carried him off within a sennight.

Several months after his brother's funeral, Sir Benedict wrote a letter to his sister-in-law, stating that he was ready to forgive her former conduct and offering her a home should she wish to remove herself and her child from their humble cottage and take up residence at Fallowfield. Mrs Leverett did not hesitate to accept this magnanimous offer, and soon she and little Portia were established in the east wing of the stately home.

'If you ask me,' Mr Chetwin concluded sourly, 'Ben always had a soft spot for the wench. I don't doubt that he intended to install her here as his mistress from the beginning. It surely was not many months after she came to live here that they resumed their former intimacy.'

'And continued in this manner until Sir Benedict's death?'

'Yes.'

'So you think that he would have winked at what was going on between you and the former governess?'

'He would have understood my needs and been tolerant.' Chetwin spread his hands. 'He could afford to be generous and, after all, it was no harm to him.'

'You are probably right. You knew him better than anyone, I expect.'

'I did, sir.'

'Thank you, Mr Chetwin.' John's words were a tacit dismissal.

'I hope that what we have said in this room will not go beyond these walls, sir,' the older man said somewhat stiffly.

'There is no need for anyone else to know of it.'

Chetwin sighed slightly, his mouth curving in a rather crooked smile.

'It's not for my sake, you understand.' He fidgeted with the fob at his waist. 'It's for her.'

'I understand perfectly.'

'As for me,' the other man concluded with great dignity, before quitting the room, 'I have nothing with which to reproach myself. I shall sleep soundly in my bed tonight. My conscience is clear.'

★ ★ ★

After his departure, both John and Lydia remained silent for almost a minute. Lydia marvelled at the absurd relations between the various inhabitants of this house, wondering whether there was any connection between them and Sir Benedict's murder. It seemed fairly certain that his niece's conduct was at least in part responsible for his presence at the temple that night. She might not have caused his death in a literal sense, but it was probable that the man would have been alive still, had he not intended to put an end to her affair.

So engrossed was she in her own thoughts that she almost forgot her husband's presence. Glancing over at him, she saw him shaking his head ever so slightly, a curious smile on his face.

'What is it, John?'

'I was thinking how inadequate is the individual conscience in discriminating between right and wrong.'

She was somewhat taken aback. 'I have been used to consider one's conscience as the only true guide in matters of morality.'

'Have you?' His smile grew. 'I fear that Dr Johnson and I must disagree with you.'

'How so?'

'Our consciences are too easily swayed by our own wishes, and even our fears. Only consider Mr Chetwin's words just now.'

'His conscience, he said, is clear.'

'Precisely.' John leaned back in the chair, surveying her across the desk. 'He has nothing but contempt for Mrs Leverett because she shared Sir Benedict's bed from what he clearly considers to be mercenary motives.'

'On the other hand,' Lydia said, following his train of thought, 'he is eager to exonerate Miss Padgett for essentially the same conduct.'

'He may have no idea of her true motives, and I suspect that he has scarcely examined his own. Yet he is quite unaware of any irony in his assertion.'

'I suppose,' Lydia said slowly, 'that we are all too apt to condemn in others what we would forgive in ourselves.'

John actually chuckled here. 'I am sure that the Grand Inquisitor slept the sleep of the innocent after torturing his victims. Why should the leopard change his spots, after all, if he is convinced that spottedness and goodness are one and the same?'

'Have we not already determined earlier that reason is not adequate to decide morality?' she complained, coming up behind him and throwing her arms about his neck. 'Must we now cast conscience as well into the flames?'

'Not at all,' he contradicted her. 'It is not that reason and conscience are unimportant, but merely that they are woefully inadequate in themselves.'

'Truth, perhaps, is not found within ourselves, but without.'

'If only,' he added, rising and pulling her to

him, 'we are willing to go in search of it, and can recognize it when we find it. For I think it rarely looks as we expect it to.'

'Meaning,' she quizzed him, 'that our present task is not likely to be an easy one?'

'I fear that it will not.'

11

A Most Suspicious Solicitor

The pursuit of truth might be a noble endeavour, but Lydia had to admit that it could be excessively fatiguing. Already she had heard enough to set her mind spinning like a carriage wheel. Yet for all its gyrations, there was no sign of progress. Perhaps they would have more luck in Ware.

Mrs Wardle-Penfield's carriage was made ready, the horses harnessed, and all in a regular train. Portia and Lydia sat side-by-side in the rear, with John facing them. It was not quite four o'clock, but the day seemed much more advanced. The drive into town took little more than half an hour, but it was almost night, and would certainly be dark long before they returned.

'I am convinced that it must have been Mr Kempton who killed my uncle,' Miss Leverett said decisively, as they pulled away from Fallowfield.

'We have no evidence as such,' John

reminded her cheerfully.

'He argued with him that very day. You said so yourself.'

This was apparently quite enough to convict the poor man, so far as this very partial young woman was concerned.

'We had best make sure the goose is well plucked before it is eaten, however,' Lydia warned with a most apt metaphor.

'Well really,' Portia asked rather tartly, 'there isn't anyone else, is there?'

'Oh, I wouldn't say that.' John looked out the window at the passing trees and hedges, a strange mix of grey and gold in the fading light. 'I wouldn't say that at all.'

'Do you mean to confront him with what you have learned?'

'I do not mean to make the attempt.'

'Well, what *do* you mean to do?'

'I shall be talking with your paramour,' he answered with bland indifference, 'while you and Lydia try if you can pry anything from the poor man.'

'Should I not go with you to see James?' Portia asked too eagerly.

'I think not.'

It was quietly spoken, but there was something about his countenance which prevented Miss Leverett from pressing the matter. Mr Savidge was a phlegmatic gentleman, to be sure, but she knew enough to hazard that he would not easily be persuaded by feminine charms.

'No, no,' Lydia said, reinforcing her husband's decree. 'I shall need your support, my dear Miss Leverett. After all, John has the advantage of us in sheer size. It will take two of us to make up for his absence, and we must at all costs appear formidable if we are to shake Mr Kempton's confidence.'

This was reasonable enough, and the young lady made no more protests during the drive. Ware was a large town, without any pretensions to be called a city. Neat and pretty, it made one welcome without encouraging one to take up residence.

The carriage soon drew up before the Kempton abode, a charming cottage with a slate roof and a neatly tended garden giving on to one of the side streets of the town. It was quite a large residence for a solicitor, in fact, giving the impression that its owner was rising in the world and not someone to be ignored.

Having been given directions by the coachman, John set off on foot, leaving them at the cottage gate. They were to collect him from the gaol after their visit.

'We are being watched,' Lydia murmured to her companion, glancing over her shoulder at the cottage just east of them. An elderly dame was standing by the low wall between the two properties, eyeing them with some interest.

'Good evening, Miss Tredlow,' Portia addressed her.

'Good evening, Miss Leverett,' came the reply, though not as cordially.

'I have an idea,' Lydia whispered to her companion. 'Introduce me to her.'

Portia was slightly taken aback, but walked the few paces across to the Kemptons' neighbour, arm-in-arm with Lydia. Miss Tredlow was not, she thought, the most amiable old lady she had ever met, but she was curious about anyone and anything which might be going forward in her small corner of the country. She was somewhat gaunt and sharp-eyed, which exactly suited Lydia's present purposes.

'So sad about your poor uncle, my dear,' the old woman said, proffering the necessary condolences.

Portia responded as conventionally as she was able, and the conversation led to an invitation to come inside for a few moments and see Miss Tredlow's mama. Miss Tredlow was a woman who was already past her three-score and ten years, and her mother must have been well over ninety. Mrs Tredlow was hard of hearing, but her daughter made little effort to compensate for this defect by raising her voice or speaking somewhat with her hands. Instead, she seemed to derive a rather macabre amusement from the situation.

'I can tell poor Mama anything,' she said with a deprecating smile, 'and it makes no difference. Is that not right, Mama?' she continued, demonstrating this. 'Is your hair not as unkempt as any scullery-maid?'

The older lady, aware that she was being addressed but having to imagine what was being said, responded, 'Oh yes, dear. But I think the lanes will be dry by tomorrow.'

Miss Tredlow shook her head, but only said to her guests, 'I can continue in this manner for hours on end. Well, at my age and in my situation, one must make whatever amusement one can.'

'We were just on our way to visit the Kemptons,' Portia said, not nearly so amused. 'I'm afraid we cannot stay very long.'

Lydia, meanwhile, recognized that a divine opportunity had presented itself.

'Poor Mr Kempton,' she said, before Miss Tredlow could say anything. 'He was actually at Fallowfield on the very day that Sir Benedict was . . . that he died.'

'Was he?' Miss Tredlow's sneer was

anything but understated. 'Too high in the instep, if you ask me,' she declared. 'Added on a room to his house last year, and keeps his own horse stabled behind, with a boy hired specially to care for it. Living above his means, while his wife plays the fine lady in town!'

She clearly was not enamoured of her neighbours, which was all to the good as far as Lydia was concerned. She would be that much more willing to spill a little scandal-broth if there was any to be spilt.

'It is a pity,' Lydia said with a sigh, 'that Mr Kempton was not at Fallowfield later that evening. He might have prevented such a dreadful occurrence. But I suppose he was at home in his bed, sound asleep.'

'That he was not!' Miss Tredlow quickly disabused her of this idea.

'No?' Lydia's air of excessive surprise might be feigned, but her curiosity was genuine.

'He left home quite early that evening, as I recall.' She nodded to herself, pursing her lips disapprovingly. 'Didn't return home until well after one o'clock in the morning either!'

'Are you sure of this, Miss Tredlow?' Portia asked, only now realizing what Lydia was about.

'Of course I'm sure! I don't sleep so well as

I used to do when I was young,' she explained. 'I was wide awake when I heard a horse trotting by on the street outside. I looked out, and watched Mr Kempton dismount and lead the animal back towards his stable.'

'You say it was after midnight, ma'am?' Lydia persisted.

'After one o'clock,' Miss Tredlow corrected her. 'I looked at the clock on the chest in my bedroom, which belonged to my poor dear papa, and it was twenty minutes past the hour.'

Lydia expressed some doubt as to whether the man Miss Tredlow had seen was truly Mr Kempton, but the old woman was quite adamant that it could have been no one else. Armed with this information, the two young women soon made their excuses and prepared to take their leave, Portia promising to call again when the weather permitted.

'Very kind of you, Miss Leverett,' Miss Tredlow answered, with a look of real pleasure. Then she turned to her mother and added, 'Miss Leverett is coming to visit us again soon, Mother. Not that it is like to be of interest to you, I daresay. You hardly know whether anyone calls or not!'

'Do you think it is so very warm, my dear?' Mrs Tredlow asked her daughter. 'I am like to freeze, myself.'

117

They departed with the sound of Miss Tredlow's sardonic laughter ringing in their ears.

'How clever you are, Lydia!' Portia exclaimed, as soon as they opened the Kemptons' front gate. 'I never would have thought of asking that old harridan anything.'

'Old tabbies have their uses, my dear,' Lydia answered cheerfully. 'But now let us see whether Mr Kempton's story will agree with hers.'

★ ★ ★

Less than five minutes later, they were ushered into the front parlour of the Kempton home, and Lydia could see what Miss Tredlow had meant by her comments about her neighbours living above their means and putting on airs. The furnishings were unusually elegant and expensive for a solicitor's residence. They were not overly ostentatious, by any means, but Lydia could see that they were of the first quality.

Mrs Kempton greeted them as though she were bestowing an honour upon them by having them there at all.

'I am so sorry that my husband is not here to see you, Miss Leverett,' she said graciously. 'He will be here directly.'

'We do not mind, do we, Miss Leverett?' Lydia said almost coyly. 'We can have a comfortable coze without any men present.'

The lady of the house called for tea, apologizing that it was all she could offer them at present, as supper would not be for another hour at least. Both her guests were happy to say that they would be gone by that time, as they were collecting Mr Savidge, and would be dining at Fallowfield in any case.

'I must have a dinner party some night, my dear Miss Leverett,' Mrs Kempton said grandly, 'and invite only the best people from Ware. Yourself and your mama, of course, will be the first to receive invitations.'

Portia's expressions of gratitude were quite insincere, but just what the lady wanted to hear. The conversation continued on quite general topics for some minutes, until the master of the house arrived and made a very gallant fuss over his two guests.

'It is not often,' he remarked, 'that we have the privilege of entertaining two such charming ladies.'

He was a man of perhaps forty, with a trim figure and punctilious manner. His hair was thinning at the crown, but still thick enough that he could not yet be described as balding. His eyes were somewhat too small, and tended to look away from one when he spoke.

Lydia did not warm to him, but she found it difficult to imagine him even holding a pistol, much less shooting someone with it.

He did not repeat his condolences to Portia, having already called on them at Fallowfield the day after the gruesome discovery. He had also been present at Sir Benedict's funeral, and gave them some details of the solemn event which ladies, naturally, were prohibited from attending.

'I understand,' he ventured presently, addressing Lydia, 'that you and your husband are conducting enquiries into Sir Benedict's murder?'

'I have asked them to try to prevent a grave miscarriage of justice, sir,' Portia answered stiffly.

'You seem very concerned about the welfare of a mere servant, Miss Leverett,' Mr Kempton said slyly, looking at a vase of flowers to her left.

'I believe, sir,' Lydia remarked in her turn, 'that you were not at home on the night Sir Benedict was shot?'

There was a moment of awkward silence, followed by an exchange of glances between husband and wife.

'You are mistaken, Mrs Savidge,' the lady of the house corrected her. 'Mr Kempton was at home all evening.'

'That is so, Mrs Kempton,' her husband said. 'I believe I had a touch of the headache that night.'

'I was at home myself, and certainly would have known if he had left the house.' Mrs Kempton's smile was perhaps a little too broad.

'But Miss Tred — ' Portia began impulsively, and was only prevented from saying more by the application of Lydia's right heel to the toes of her left foot. She gave a slight squeal, but said no more.

'Indeed?' Lydia wondered aloud. 'How strange. But it is fortunate that you did not go out, sir. It might have seemed rather . . . suspicious . . . if you had been abroad at the time.'

'How so?' the gentleman demanded, suddenly on the offensive. 'I could have had no reason to want Sir Benedict dead!'

'It is of no consequence, I am sure.' Lydia was all solicitude. 'But you *were* heard arguing with Sir Benedict that very afternoon, you know.'

'It is a barefaced lie!' Kempton, looking out of the window, actually got to his feet at this. 'I was on the best of terms with the old man. Never a cross word between us.'

'Perhaps it was someone else, then,' Lydia shrugged.

'Who has told you this?'

'Oh, several people overheard y — some- one arguing with him,' Lydia lied glibly. 'Angry voices do tend to carry, do they not?'

'I was not angry that afternoon, ma'am.'

'No? I wonder, then, that you rode away in such a hurry.'

He was now absolutely trembling, though with rage rather than fear. His gaze was everywhere at once.

'I know not who your informant might be, Mrs Savidge,' he said between clenched teeth, 'but they seem to be suffering from a highly romantic imagination.'

'And did you know, sir,' Lydia gave another turn of the screw, 'that Sir Benedict had written a new will on the evening of his death?'

'What!' His astonishment was great, but undoubtedly real.

She explained what John had discovered in the dead man's desk, which temporarily distracted him from her previous suggestions. His legal instincts were aroused, and he assured them both that the will was almost certainly invalid.

'Though I cannot believe that Sir Benedict would really disinherit you, Miss Leverett.' He shook his head, and actually looked directly at her for a moment. 'Can you think

122

of any reason why he would want to do such a thing?'

'Not at all.' The lie tripped off her tongue very easily, Lydia noted. Miss Portia Leverett would have no trouble concealing the truth when it suited her.

They remained only a few more minutes, and could not doubt that their host and hostess were as eager for them to be gone as they were eager to leave. It had not been a comfortable visit, but a very revealing one.

12

The Handsome Captive

While the two women were crowing over their success in uncovering a significant clue to their mystery, John was engaged in conversation with Mr James Bromley. Initially he had been met by the gaoler, Mr Noyes, with rather less than encouragement. When it was made clear to him, however, that this strange visitor was the son of a Justice of the Peace and a friend of Miss Leverett, he was quite as impressed as if one of the royal dukes had presented himself.

'Of course, sir,' Mr Noyes said, almost bowing in his reverence for the gentleman's station. 'I will take you in directly, sir.'

'You are too kind.' John's lips twitched ever so slightly, though he managed to maintain an otherwise cool countenance.

The gaol was a small stone building with only a few cells where malefactors could be held while awaiting their fate. Mercifully, it was relatively clean, the only smell coming from one or two of those incarcerated there, who were desperately in need of washing.

Mr Noyes took his keys and opened a very solid door with a grate in it, allowing John to pass through before him. In the dim light of the interior, he could see a tall, slim figure with a thatch of golden-brown locks. At the moment, the man's head was bent, his shoulders hunched in a manner which seemed to betoken abject misery. When he looked up, however, the impression was dispelled. The gentleman was even younger than John had imagined: not more than twenty, he'd wager. With twinkling blue eyes and a determined set to his jaw, he seemed remarkably sanguine, considering his circumstances, and not at all dejected.

'James Bromley?' John asked, extending his hand in greeting.

'Aye,' the lad stood and reached out to shake John's hand. 'And who might you be, sir?'

John introduced himself and explained that he had come at the request of Miss Leverett, at which the young man's hesitation vanished. He asked eagerly how Portia was, his eyes almost literally lighting up at the mention of her name. Clearly he was quite besotted with the girl, and John thought it best to dismiss Mr Noyes before Mr Bromley could say too much.

As soon as they were left alone, he came straight to the point: 'Miss Leverett has asked my wife and me to look into this matter, to see if we can discover who killed her uncle.'

'I knew she wouldn't let me down, sir,' James Bromley said with absolute confidence. 'She's the most resourceful lass!'

He then wasted several precious minutes listing the many endearing qualities of Miss Leverett, which were of absolutely no interest to John; but he thought it best to let him get it over with at once so that they might proceed more rationally thereafter.

'Did you know that Sir Benedict was aware of your liaison with Miss Leverett?' he asked first.

'My what, sir?'

'Did Sir Benedict know that you were meeting his niece in secret?'

'I never thought so, sir, though I suppose he must've, seeing as how he went to the temple that night. I mean, why else would he have been there?'

'As you say,' John murmured. 'But neither you nor Portia had any idea that he knew?'

'Oh no, sir. I can't believe it myself,' he added, frowning. 'I mean, I don't know why he didn't send me packing at once.'

'Very likely that is what he meant to do at

the temple. It seems reasonable to suppose that he had only learned of your rendezvous that day.'

'My what, sir?'

'Never mind.' John smiled to himself, thinking that his language was becoming a little too refined. 'What I want you to do is to tell me all you can remember from the time you went to meet Miss Leverett that evening.'

What followed was basically what he had already heard from Portia. James had slipped away from the stables after midnight — he wasn't sure of the exact time — and made his way towards the temple. The path led from the other side of the house from that which Portia had taken, and he had neither seen nor heard anything until the sound of a gun being fired had startled him.

'I just stopped dead still for a moment,' he admitted. 'Couldn't think what to do. Then I ran for the temple, 'cause it sounded like it came from that direction.'

When he arrived at the temple a few minutes later, Portia was already there, kneeling beside her uncle's body. Her face, when she looked up at him, was milk white in the moonlight, and he knew at once that the man lying beside her was dead.

'I almost thought for a minute that she had done it herself,' James confessed, a little shamefaced. 'But I know she couldn't do such a thing, not Portia!'

John himself would not have been so confident. Privately, he considered that Miss Leverett was capable of almost anything. But he nodded his assent and let the man continue. There was not much more to tell, however. His sweetheart urged him to return to the stables while she raised the alarm, but he insisted on accompanying her back to the house. After all, whoever killed Sir Benedict might still be lurking in the grounds, and it was not likely he would allow his beloved to risk being murdered herself.

Naturally, everyone wanted to know what Miss Leverett had been doing wandering about at such a time of night. It was not very long before rumours — from the servants, it was to be understood — led the authorities to uncover the reprehensible conduct of the young heiress and to discover the identity of her lover. It was a nine days' wonder, and the talk of the town, though nobody would ever close their doors to Sir Benedict's niece.

'I understand that you are an artist, Mr Bromley,' John said somewhat more gently.

'Not a *real* artist, sir,' he answered with some self-deprecation, 'though the drawing master who gave me lessons said I was gifted. My father thought it all nonsense, however, and refused to let me have more lessons.'

'Your father was mistaken, James,' John said, with more certainty than he had expressed thus far. 'One of my friends is the son of a member of the Royal Academy. I shall speak to him and see if we can ensure that your talent is not wasted.'

'Thank you, sir!' His gratitude was quite embarrassing, and John quickly reverted to their former discussion.

'Can you recall anything, anything at all, about that evening that struck you as unusual at the time?' he asked.

James Bromley's brow furrowed in an effort of concentration, as he conscientiously attempted to follow his instructions.

'Well, Mr Savidge,' he said at length, 'there was one thing I thought was peculiar at the time, but I don't think it means anything.'

'Let me be the judge of that,' John told him. 'What was it, James?'

⋆   ⋆   ⋆

'He is guilty, I'm sure of it!' Portia announced as soon as they entered the carriage.

Lydia laughed out loud at her willingness to convict the gentleman. She would probably condemn Christ and His twelve Apostles to save her precious James.

'I would not convict him quite so hastily,' she cautioned when she had gained control of herself. 'But either Mr Kempton or Miss Tredlow is lying. I'm inclined to doubt the former.'

'Of course he's lying! His wife too. I never did like her.'

They drew away from the house rather slowly, and Lydia commented, 'I hope that John has had equal luck with Mr Bromley.'

'James cannot have much to say. He knows nothing about my uncle's death, of that I am certain.'

'He saw the body,' Lydia pointed out. 'He might recall something which escaped your notice.'

'That may be,' she conceded doubtfully. Then, with sudden intensity, she continued, 'Oh, Lydia, I am so miserable without my James! I would give my soul to taste his lips once more, to have his arms about me and to feel the warmth of his body against mine!'

Lydia blinked at this, but could think of nothing to say. Aunt Camilla, she thought, might appreciate such a speech — though even she would be scandalized by Miss Leverett's behaviour as an unmarried woman who was carrying a stable boy's love-child.

'I hope,' she ventured at last, 'that we will be able to restore Mr Bromley to you.'

'He is my world, Lydia. He is my life!'

'Quite.'

'Do you not desire Mr Savidge more than food or drink?' Portia eyed her with some misgiving.

'Well, not at suppertime at least.'

'Do be serious!' she protested. 'I cannot imagine life without James. Is not the passion between man and woman the purest, most noble thing on earth?'

'I cannot say that it is,' Lydia replied honestly.

'But does not your body ache and burn for your lover's touch when you are apart?'

'Not at all.' She could see that Portia was shocked by her attitude, and added, 'Of course, I have scarcely been apart from John at all since our wedding. I would certainly miss him if we were separated for any length of time.'

'Even a day apart is agony when one is in love!'

'Is it?'

'Oh, you cannot be truly in love, Lydia, if you have not felt the divine union of two souls which makes parting unendurable.' She drew a deep breath before continuing with grim deliberation, 'I would kill anyone who tried to come between me and my love.'

On the whole, Lydia was thankful that at

this moment they arrived at the street beside the gaol. John was standing on the pavement, looking as unconcerned as always, and she did indeed feel something of the joy which Miss Leverett had just described — although it was more in the nature of gratitude for being rescued from her companion's evangelical fervour. She began to wonder whether the young woman might indeed have murdered her uncle rather than be separated from Mr Bromley. Romantic love was far too closely allied with undisciplined emotion for her to be entirely comfortable with it.

★   ★   ★

'John!' Lydia cried as he entered the carriage. 'We have so much to tell you.'

'Do you, my dear?' he asked, smiling indulgently.

'How is my dearest James?' Miss Leverett leaned forward, almost pleading in her anxiety. 'Is he well? Has he been barbarously used?'

'Under the circumstances, he looks remarkably well.'

Portia was clearly not satisfied with this response. No doubt she had been hoping to hear that James was wasting away, nearly mad with fear and half-dead from longing for his love. There was a decided degree of selfishness about this sort of 'true love', Lydia considered. It seemed designed to elevate the consciousness of the lover more than it betokened any genuine regard for the beloved. She had had quite enough of it for the moment, and eagerly returned to the business at hand.

'Let me tell you what we have discovered.'

'By all means,' John said.

After detailing what Miss Tredlow had told them, Lydia went on to recount the details of their interview with Mr and Mrs Kempton.

'No doubt Mrs Kempton is lying in order to protect her husband from suspicion.'

'That is my supposition.'

'I would like to speak with Kempton myself.' John's quiet tone belied his determination, Lydia knew. 'Perhaps you might invite Mr and Mrs Kempton to take their mutton at Fallowfield tomorrow evening, Miss Leverett?'

'If you think it necessary.'

Portia seemed to speak at random, scarcely attending to what was being said. She was in a brown study, to be sure.

'Are you quite well?' Lydia asked her, not certain whether she was more concerned or annoyed at her attitude.

'I do not see,' she declared, slouching in

her corner of the carriage, 'what use any of this might be.'

'Perhaps none,' John admitted without apology. 'We are merely trying to collect as much information as we are able, in the hope that something may come to light which might exonerate Mr Bromley and bring the real killer to justice.'

'But what has been accomplished so far?' she demanded.

'We already have another strong candidate for murder in Mr Kempton,' he pointed out. 'And I have learned something very interesting from your James.'

13

A Coat of Bloody Colour

'Do tell us, John!' Lydia exclaimed, suddenly all excitement. This was much more promising.

'Learned something from James?' Portia echoed, rather surprised.

'Remember' — John leaned back in his seat, surveying them both through the semi-gloom — 'that I asked you if there was nothing about that evening which struck you as . . . odd?'

'Yes. But I really cannot think of anything.'

'But James did.'

'Well, what was it?'

'Why,' John asked in turn, 'was your uncle not wearing a greatcoat?'

'What?'

'According to Mr Bromley, when he arrived at the temple Sir Benedict — or rather, Sir Benedict's corpse — was clad only in evening breeches and a light dress coat. And it was,' he added pointedly, 'quite a chilly evening.'

Portia tilted her head, her eyes opening wide as she cast her mind back. For a moment she was silent, and then burst out, 'He is quite right, of course! Now that you mention it, he was not dressed very warmly. But I do not see how that can be of any significance.'

Lydia had to agree with Miss Leverett on this point. Not everyone is equally sensitive to the elements, after all, and what one person might consider a cold evening, another would find pleasantly refreshing.

'It might mean nothing,' John conceded. 'Or it might be of the utmost importance.'

'It is curious indeed,' Lydia conceded. 'But hardly — '

'Do you know where your uncle's greatcoat might be?' John interrupted, which she did not like at all.

'I suppose it is hanging in the alcove at the end of the lower hall, with the others.'

'The others?'

Lydia was glad that he asked this question, which was precisely what she herself was about to do. Had Sir Benedict possessed a collection of coats?

'My uncle was ever a man of strict order,' the girl explained, 'who insisted upon everything being ship-shape as they say.'

However he had come by the habit, Lydia

and John discovered that it was one of Sir Benedict's most consistent — and irritating — characteristics. Everything in his house was done according to a strict regimen which must be adhered to faithfully. Servants were instructed to perform specific tasks at prescribed times and on certain days only: the butler polished the silver on Fridays, between noon and six in the evening precisely; every bed in the house was turned on Tuesday mornings; Sir Benedict himself attended to the household accounts only on Thursdays, never beginning before ten o'clock in the morning.

As for the coats, he had made use of a small niche at the back of the house, perhaps six feet in width and three feet deep. Here he had decreed that the coats, capes and other such garments of every inmate at Fallowfield should be hung on pegs projecting from the wall. This way, they were ever accessible when required, but in nobody's way.

'I must admit,' Portia stated somewhat grudgingly, 'that it is most efficient.'

By now they had arrived at the house, and John requested that she show them precisely where the coats were kept. Though she continued to express doubt as to the necessity of such an enterprise, she led them to a back door which opened into the kitchen. Cook, somewhat surprised, greeted her kindly enough, though Lydia heard her mutter under her breath about spoilt meals resulting from folks coming home at all hours and such.

'Here is the place,' Portia announced at last, flinging out an arm to indicate the niche in the wall.

Peering into it, Lydia immediately saw that it was, as she had said, a very sensible arrangement. A row of greatcoats and cloaks filled the wall at the back, each one easily reached although not protruding into the room itself.

'You see,' Portia informed them, pointing, 'there is Jenkins's old coat, then Winny's box coat, then my uncle's . . . and then Mama's and mine.'

The first three she indicated were clearly men's greatcoats, all rather similar. The butler's was perhaps more shabby, probably having been handed down from his master when it had seen better years. Mr Chetwin's coat was virtually identical to Sir Benedict's, though the cuffs were a trifle less deep and it had three shoulder capes where the other man's sported four.

'Let me see.' John reached in and pulled Sir Benedict's coat towards him. Almost as soon as it was in his hand, Lydia noticed something.

'What is that?' She pointed to several dark spots marring the right sleeve, from the cuff to just below the elbow.

'I would say,' John answered, lifting the garment up to his face, 'that it is very likely Sir Benedict's blood.'

'Blood!' the two women cried in unison.

'Almost certainly.'

Lydia felt a jolt of pure excitement as she looked at the speckled sleeve with its spots scarcely noticeable on the dark wool. Closer inspection revealed another, larger stain near the hem of the garment — possibly, John conjectured, where the body had fallen against it on its way to the floor of the temple. Here was something at last!

'How clever of James to have noticed the coat's absence.' Portia preened as though she had thought of it herself.

'He has the artist's eye for detail,' Lydia said.

'But if my uncle was not wearing his coat, how did his blood come to be on it?'

'Clearly someone else must have — Ooh!' Lydia's speech was cut short by a particularly painful pinch upon her upper arm, delivered without pity by her own husband.

'What on earth is the matter, Lydia?' the other girl looked at her in surprise, having completely missed the gentleman's most improper action.

Lydia glanced briefly at John, who was frowning heavily, and who gave a turn of the head so slight that only she was aware of this decidedly negative gesture. Correctly interpreting it as a desire for her to refrain from saying more in front of their esteemed patroness, Lydia drew a slight breath before continuing.

'Pray excuse me,' she ventured at last. 'A stitch in my side, probably because I have not yet eaten.'

'But you were about to say something,' Miss Leverett reminded her.

'Was I?' She cudgelled her imagination, attempting to master it sufficiently to produce something reasonable, but with indifferent results. 'I merely meant to say that somehow or other the blood must have got on to the sleeve.'

Portia gave her a look which indicated that she was beginning to doubt the intellect of her new acquaintance. She had no opportunity to respond to this fatuous observation, however, being forestalled by John.

'I think we had all better attend to our supper,' he said, with his usual quiet good humour. 'I shall think on this tonight, and perhaps we can make some sense of it. In the meantime, I think it best if you do not mention this discovery to anyone, Miss Leverett.'

'Very well.' The young lady was dubious but acquiescent. 'It scarcely seems worth mentioning, after all.'

'But may I ask,' John said, directing her attention to his right, 'where that flight of stairs might lead?'

The stairs he mentioned were but a few paces to their left at the rear of the hallway where they stood, narrow and steep and tucked away so as to be quite out of notice of anyone who did not venture to the very back of the house.

'They lead to the rooms above,' she informed them. 'It is merely for the convenience of the servants, that they might have access without being in anybody's way.'

'It is nothing unusual in such a large residence,' Lydia pointed out.

'No indeed.' John smiled quizzically. 'In fact, I was just thinking that we might also use them so as to be out of everyone's way, my dear.'

'Do you not mean to go in to supper?'

'Supper will already be over, I'm afraid,' Portia said, with grim certainty. 'We stayed too late in Ware, and Mama would never allow the food to grow cold waiting for us.'

'Nor did I expect as much.'

'Certainly not,' Lydia added, not wishing to seem importunate.

'I shall have one of the servants bring something up to you, if you do not mind it.'

'*I* should not mind it in the least,' Lydia said, with some relief, since she really was very hungry.

'We should be most grateful, Miss Leverett.'

14

In the Footsteps of a Killer

Lydia and John ascended the steps with a lighted taper guiding them through the darkness. As they reached the top, John let out a sudden cry. This was due to the fact that Lydia had just pinched him very sharply upon his exposed hand.

'That was quite unnecessary, my dear,' he said, recovering himself almost immediately. His cry had been more from surprise than pain, in any case.

'And I suppose it was necessary to bruise my arm so unmercifully?' she returned.

'It was the only thing I could think of at that moment.'

'The next time you wish me to be silent, please have the grace to think of something more original — and less painful!' she snapped.

'Shall I beg your forgiveness, my sweet?'

'Now you are roasting me!'

'Never.'

They had reached the door of their bedchamber, and he opened it for her to precede him.

'Why,' she demanded, crossing the threshold and turning to confront him as he closed the door, 'did you not wish me to speak before Portia?'

'Miss Leverett is a clever miss.' He took her arm and led her to the bed, pulling her down beside him. 'It will not be long before she understands the significance of that coat, but let us not hurry her.'

'It is completely incomprehensible.' Lydia shook her head. 'Sir Benedict was shot by someone who was wearing his own greatcoat! But why?'

'If I knew the *why* of the matter, I suppose it would be no great task to discover the *who*.' John sighed slightly. 'But alas, I am as puzzled as anyone.'

'What do you think of James Bromley?' Lydia asked her husband, turning the subject.

John gave the matter some consideration before replying.

'He seems a very plain-spoken, honest young man — and very much in love with Miss Leverett.'

'Is his love genuine, do you think?'

'Oh, unquestionably. He seems quite overwhelmed by her condescension in loving 'one so far beneath her.'

'He sounds like an ass to me. Is he?'

'Love makes an ass of most men, and he is very young.'

'A young ass is the most tiresome of all. They bray rather too loudly and long.'

'And Miss Portia?' John enquired with a raised eyebrow. 'She must have strong feelings for the young man.'

'She does,' Lydia assured him. 'She has conceived the most violent passion for him.'

'Oh.'

He said no more, but it was more than enough.

'What do you mean by that curious monosyllable?'

'Only that violent passion should never be confused with love.'

'Violent passion may grow into love, surely?'

'It has been known to happen.' John leaned back upon the bed, half reclining upon his elbows. 'But I think it is not common. More often, violent passion dwindles first into contempt, and finally into utter indifference which is the very opposite of love.'

Lydia considered the matter, deciding that John was correct as usual. Love should grow slowly and quietly, like a seed planted in the earth, not dropped into the sea like a coconut, to be washed up at last on some uncharted shore.

'Our most promising piece of news, then,' she said, reverting to their real business here, 'has been the evidence of Miss Tredlow.'

'Mr Kempton would certainly seem to be our man, on the face of it.'

'He had ample reason for wanting Sir Benedict dead, if he was unable to repay his debts to him,' Lydia began.

'And it appears that he also had a perfect opportunity that night to ride over to Fallowfield, tether his horse to a nearby tree, and waylay Sir Benedict at the temple.'

'It fits as neatly as a glove.'

'Perhaps too neatly,' John warned.

'How vexatious!' Lydia cried. 'I feel precisely as you do, but I cannot account for my doubts.'

John, however, could more logically present the obstacles involved. Why, for example, would Mr Kempton risk entering the house and donning the coat belonging to his intended victim? One of the servants might easily have discovered him and raised the alarm.

'He may have meant to disguise himself as Sir Benedict, in the event he was seen walking about the park.'

But John would have none of it. It was unlikely, he said, that anyone would have confronted him upon the grounds face to face. And in the faint moonlight, seen from a distance, nobody was likely to have recognized him, whatever his apparel.

'No,' he said flatly. 'It is quite absurd.'

Most difficult of all to resolve, however, was the one question which applied to everyone at Fallowfield, as well as to the solicitor. It seemed that Sir Benedict had confided in no one his intention of confronting his niece and her lover at their favourite rendezvous.

'Nobody at all seems to have known that he would be there on that evening.'

'Somebody must have known,' Lydia pointed out.

'It may be,' John said, thinking aloud, 'that someone saw Sir Benedict slip from the house and guessed what he was about. They followed him to the temple and killed him there, but it was a crime quite unplanned and unconsidered beforehand.'

'It was very foolish too.' Lydia lay back upon the pillows, watching John with furrowed brows. 'If the killer knew that Portia and Mr Bromley would be meeting there as well, there was a very good chance that he, or she, would be seen by one of them.'

'And the question yet remains: why dress in Sir Benedict's coat?'

They were back where they began. The discovery of the bloodstained coat seemed only to make everything more incomprehensible than ever.

At that moment, there was a knock upon the door. It was opened by Bridget, a pert and pretty housemaid whom Lydia had noticed eyeing John with some deliberation earlier in the day.

The girl carried a tray of enticing victuals in her hands: two plates with cold ham, bread, mustard and boiled potatoes; two bowls of soup made from portions of lamb and vegetables, and two glasses of wine.

Lydia hurried Bridget away as fast as possible, and she and John set-to on the food which her stomach had been anticipating for some time. Simple but filling, they were both well satisfied and, after consuming everything on the tray but the china and silverware, they extinguished the taper, lay down upon the bed and fell into a comfortable doze. It was no wonder if they were fagged to death after such a day as this had been!

★   ★   ★

Lydia awoke with a start and looked around her. The room was dark, except for the cool grey moonlight falling upon them through the window. It was, as the clock informed her, some twenty minutes after midnight.

It suddenly occurred to her that this was about the time that Portia had been traipsing about in search of a romantic encounter, and found her uncle's corpse instead. On impulse, Lydia sat up and moved her legs over the side of the bed. Beside her, John emitted a gentle snore.

Should she wake him? It seemed too cruel. In any case, he might think her sudden resolution absurd. It would be just like him, she thought, to rein in her imagination just as it was about to gallop away with her. Well, not tonight! Common sense was all very well, but she was in the mood for a little adventure.

Very cautiously, she opened the door of the bedchamber, peering down the darkened hallway. All was completely still, but her eyes were growing accustomed to the darkness and she inched her way around the frame and out into the passage without so much as a rustle to betray her.

With some trepidation, she made her way to the stairs up which they had come earlier. Though she was no coward, she had to own to a slight feeling of apprehension as she made her way down, for it was pitch-dark in the stairwell and she had to feel her way with utmost caution, testing each step with her foot as she went.

Arriving the bottom at last, she reached out into the alcove. Recalling that the ladies' cloaks were hung to the right, she extracted one — whether belonging to Portia, her mama, or Miss Padgett, she could not tell — and headed towards the kitchen.

This room was full of ominous shadows and strange shapes, but the door was quite easy to find, even in the gloom. An instant later and she was outside, glad of the warm folds of the pelisse. She turned at once in the direction of the temple and started to walk, slowly at first, and then with increasing confidence.

Though the moon was not now full, it was a clear enough night that her path was relatively easy to follow. She had passed a low thicket and lost sight of the house, when she heard a slight noise which could only be the crunch of feet upon the gravel.

For a moment she paused. The sound ceased. But she knew that it was not her own steps she had heard. She moved on. The sound began again. In spite of herself, her heart began to pound harder and faster than was customary.

Quickening her pace, she moved on, her mind awhirl with ominous possibilities. Someone had seen her leave the house. Someone was following. Could it be the same person who had followed Sir Benedict to the temple so recently? Was there a pistol clutched in their hand even now?

Her breath was coming faster, her steps almost a run while the crunch-crunch behind her grew ever nearer. She dared not look behind, dared not falter in her course . . .

Suddenly, like a heavy sack flung across her back, a large hand descended upon her shoulder from behind. She stopped at once, her breath escaping her in a rush. Then, refusing to acknowledge the sudden fear which gripped her, she spun about to face her attacker.

'John!'

Her voice was not as assured as she had hoped it would be. But this, though far less terrifying than the apparition she had expected, was disconcerting enough. It was especially annoying to see the flash of white teeth in the moonlight and to realize that he was very much enjoying her discomfiture.

'Whom are you planning to meet at the Temple of the Seven Virtues, Mrs Savidge?' he asked.

'My husband, of course,' she returned, her courage restored, along with her wit. 'I wondered how long it would take you to find me.'

'Well played, madam wife.' He sketched a quick bow.

'How *did* you manage to find me?' she asked now, abandoning further pretence.

He chuckled softly. 'I awoke from sleep, only to observe you slipping out of the door like a thief. What could I do but follow?'

'I wanted to see for myself how easy it would be to get out of the house and make my way to the temple unobserved.'

'An excellent idea,' he said, surprising her with his quick acceptance. 'May I be permitted to assist you in this endeavour?'

'By all means.'

They continued on their way, this time arm-in-arm. It was, in truth, a lovely night, if less than balmy. The chill was just enough to merit a coat, and Lydia rather suspected that it was remarkably similar to what it must have been the evening that Sir Benedict died.

At length the temple rose up out of the grass as they crested the small hillock before it. It looked particularly eerie in the moonlight, more pagan than Christian as they approached the portal.

'Now,' John announced, 'you shall play the part of Sir Benedict, and I will be the killer.'

'Perhaps I might wish to be the killer,' Lydia protested.

'Very well.'

'No,' she said, changing her mind. 'You would make a far better murderer than I.'

'Thank you.'

She gave a comical grimace, but offered no comment. John therefore went into the building and stationed himself behind the door and to the right. Lydia waited a moment before entering. Although she knew that she would find him standing there, his large form blending with the even darker shadows lent such an air of menace to the place that she shivered involuntarily. It was altogether a cold place, she thought. Virtue should not be so chill.

'He would have been shot as soon as he came through.' Though there was no need for it, she found herself whispering.

'Undoubtedly.' John pointed his finger at her head and pretended to fire an imaginary pistol. 'The body would have fallen at his feet immediately, I imagine. The killer then simply exited and ran back towards the house.'

'When one thinks of it,' Lydia said slowly, 'it is remarkable that he encountered nobody else.'

'With so many wandering about, you mean?'

'Precisely.'

'Well,' John commented, as they made their own way back, rather more slowly than the murderer would have, 'we have at least proved that one can accomplish the deed without being observed.'

'I thought that we had proved just the opposite,' she countered wryly, 'since you very quickly found me out, sir.'

'But I was sharing your bed, and could hardly help but notice your absence from it.'

'With so many people in this house sharing someone else's bed, it is hard to believe that on that one night everyone was quite alone.'

'Which makes it all the more difficult to determine who is most likely to have done the deed.'

'It must be Mr Kempton,' she insisted.

By now they had reached the kitchen door, and entered it as easily as they had left.

'I wish I could believe so.'

'As do I.'

In the end, it was determined that all that could be done now was to sleep. Perhaps, John suggested, they might dream the solution to the crime.

'I wish Papa was here,' Lydia muttered. 'I know he would be able to help us.'

'He certainly proved invaluable before,' John conceded. 'But we must learn to tackle these things on our own.'

'Do you think that we can?'

'Surely you and I can do anything we set our minds to?' he countered.

'We shall soon see if that is true.'

15

A Much Too Merry Maid

In the morning, they began again. After breakfast, which they shared with a glowering Mr Chetwin and a shivering Miss Padgett, John decided that there was nothing for it but to begin questioning the servants.

The cook, Mrs Morven, had nothing to remark beyond the various culinary tastes of each member of the household, which seemed to be the only thing of interest to her. The stable hands were mystified, but unanimous in declaring that James Bromley was the least likely of lads to kill anyone. That, at least, must count for something — though not of the kind to save the poor fellow from the gibbet.

It was not until they interviewed Mr Jenkins, the butler, that anything of note was uncovered. When asked whether something unusual had occurred on the day of Sir Benedict's murder, he hesitated a moment before revealing that he had overheard Sir

Benedict in a heated argument with someone. John immediately assumed that it must have been the same fracas with Mr Kempton which had already been related by the gardener. Jenkins soon disabused him of this notion, however.

'I could not hear what was being said,' he commented with majestic disdain, 'but I cannot help but be surprised that she is still with us.'

'She?' John leapt upon the word like a cat upon a cornered mouse. Lydia, whose attention had begun to wander, was immediately recalled to herself.

'Bridget, sir.'

'Bridget?'

'Bridget Pollard,' Jenkins explained. 'The upper housemaid.'

Of course! Lydia remembered Bridget well. She was the very maid who had brought them their supper on the previous evening. Lydia did not like her. She was a little too *séduisante* for any young wife to be comfortable with her.

'You say that your master argued with this maid?' John was asking now.

'Yes, sir.'

'But you do not know what the argument was about?'

'No, sir.'

'Very good, Jenkins.' John shot a glance at Lydia, which clearly conveyed to her that here was yet another morsel of highly interesting information.

Jenkins rose from his seat. 'Will that be all, sir?'

John nodded his assent. 'You have been most helpful. But would you be so good as to send Bridget in to us?'

'Certainly, sir.' The smile which flickered briefly across his face was one of pure satisfaction.

'I think that the butler is not one of Miss Bridget's admirers,' Lydia commented drily as he exited.

'No.' John stared at the closed door. 'He means to make mischief. But I do not believe that he would lie in order to do so. He may be using his information to avenge some impertinence on her part, perhaps, but I'd wager that he has told nothing but the truth.'

★ ★ ★

Lydia settled herself more comfortably in her chair at the side of the desk and waited for Bridget's arrival. It was not many minutes before there was a respectful knock at the door. Immediately upon John's call to enter, the door opened, and there she was, as pert and pretty as Lydia remembered.

'You called for me, sir?' she asked, smiling directly at John and giving only the most cursory nod to his wife.

'I understand from Mr Jenkins,' John said, coming directly to the point, 'that you had words with your master on the day of his death.'

'Told you that, did he?' Bridget's mouth compressed into a thin line, her sharp eyes glinting with barely suppressed ire. 'Worse than an old woman, 'e is.'

'*Did* you quarrel with Sir Benedict that day?' Lydia queried, already beginning to lose patience with the girl.

'What if I did?' Bridget glanced at her, none too pleased, she suspected, at being interrogated by one of her own sex. Though only a year or two older than Lydia, she was a girl with an instinctive knowledge of how to handle men, but females generally disliked her. For good reason, Lydia imagined.

'What precipitated the quarrel, Miss Pollard?' John demanded.

'What?' She looked momentarily mystified.

'What did you argue about?' Lydia asked more plainly.

Thick eyelashes descended, veiling big blue eyes which seemed to indicate a sudden attack of unwonted shyness.

'I don't know as I should say, sir.' The lashes fluttered coquettishly. 'It's a bit of a delicate matter, you might say.'

'You had been caught at something,' Lydia interrupted harshly. She was not impressed by the young lady's charms. 'What was it, girl?'

The fluttering stopped, to be replaced by a hard look which Lydia thought was more natural to Bridget Pollard. She was undoubtedly a calculating wench, but she would find that Mrs John Savidge was not so easily cozened as the gentlemen with whom she was acquainted.

'You see, sir,' Bridget once more directed her words to John, 'Sir Caleb had come over that morning to see Miss Portia. But she was out riding, or so she said.'

These last words indicated the maid's opinion of Miss Leverett's veracity, but both Lydia and John thought it best to let it pass. Instead, they encouraged Miss Pollard to relate exactly what happened that morning.

It was common knowledge, they were given to understand, that Sir Caleb Hovington had every intention of marrying Miss Leverett. Not only was she an attractive young woman, but the heiress of Fallowfield. From his point of view, the match could hardly be any more suitable. Sir Benedict had encouraged his

159

suit, from reasons which were practical enough, but scarcely calculated to persuade a romantic young lady of one-and-twenty.

Portia's aversion to Sir Caleb had not gone unnoticed, but the gentleman preferred to ignore her lack of enthusiasm and to ascribe it to maidenly modesty — a quality which Lydia very much doubted that Portia had ever possessed.

But while his intentions were honourable and his courtship perfectly serious, he was, after all, a man of the world; and if the young lady he sought as his wife was not inclined to gratify his matrimonial desires, there were other young women who could at least satisfy his more earthy appetites. One of those, as it happened, was well within arm's reach: Miss Bridget Pollard, housemaid, to be more exact. Sir Caleb was not above an enjoyable kiss and cuddle with the girl, when the opportunity arose, which he made sure that it did with some frequency.

'We was behind the stairs that morning,' Bridget said unblushingly, 'not expectin' anyone to be spyin' on us. It was just a little fun — nothin' special, if you know what I mean.'

John knew precisely what she meant, and Lydia was now woman enough to understand the essentials.

'And Sir Benedict,' John pressed her, 'discovered you in Sir Caleb's . . . embrace?'

'That's it, sir!' Bridget was pleased at his perspicacity. 'And he wasn't none too pleased, I can tell you. The things he called me . . . ' Her brow darkened and her lips pursed at the memory.

'And what of Sir Caleb?' Lydia could not help asking. 'Did Sir Benedict not call him to book as well?'

'Lord, ma'am!' Bridget's laughter was spontaneous and quite genuine. 'He didn't stay long enough to hear more than two words from Sir Ben. Loped off so fast, he looked like one of them elfants from Africa I've heard about, runnin' through the jungle!'

'So you received the brunt of Sir Benedict's animosity?'

'Beg pardon, sir?'

'You had to face your master's anger alone,' Lydia elucidated John's words, adding, 'Were you not ashamed of being caught in such a position with your neighbour . . . and Miss Leverett's suitor?'

'What would I be ashamed for?' Bridget demanded fiercely. 'She don't want the old fool. No!' She sniffed contemptuously. 'Not Miss Portia. Too busy stealing other girls' men from 'em — and not even one of her own class! That'd be too easy for her, I suppose.'

Light began to dawn. It seemed that Miss Leverett was not the only young woman who found James Bromley attractive. No indeed.

'You saw nothing wrong in allowing Sir Caleb to kiss you upon occasion, then?'

'I allowed him a great deal more'n that,' she admitted.

'Do you expect Sir Caleb to marry you, Miss Pollard?' Lydia could not resist asking.

Another burst of laughter was the response to this question. 'Lord, you do say the funniest things! Not much chance of a man of Quality like him marrying a girl like me, is it?' She shrugged, accepting the reality of her world. 'But if I play me cards right, I could be taken care of well enough, and not have to spend me life scrubbin' and cleanin'. I ain't goin' to end my days as somebody's servant, I promise you.'

Lydia believed her. There was a hardness and a determination about her which were quite formidable. She would make her way in the world, undoubtedly. She might have to abandon all that was decent and human to do so, but that would be no difficult task. She had already relieved herself of a great deal of moral baggage.

'But you have not told us the most important thing, my dear,' John reverted to the subject at hand.

'What's that, sir?'

'Why did not Sir Benedict dismiss you immediately?'

A sly look came into her face. 'Oh, he was all ready to send me packing,' she admitted. 'Until I let him know that his own niece wasn't no better than I am.'

'You told him about Miss Leverett and James Bromley?'

'Told him to his face how Jim was givin' Miss Portia the green gown every chance he had, down at the temple in the park.' Her mouth twisted in something which was too bitter to be a smile. 'She wasn't the first girl he took there, neither. I can swear to that!'

Lydia caught her breath.

'He did not know of his niece's affair before this?'

'From the look on 'is face when I told 'im, I'd say he didn't.' She looked quite proud at her accomplishment. 'Just as blind, in his way, as Mr Chetwin.'

She continued by saying that she had really 'tipped the old man a doubler'. He pretended not to believe her, but she knew he was just shamming. He turned away, striding down the hall and calling over his shoulder that he would deal with her on the morrow.

'But the next day,' John said slowly, 'he was dead.'

'That's it.' She nodded. 'And I wasn't going to be the one to mention that he was planning to throw me out — not but what I'm sure I could've persuaded Sir Caleb to give me shelter.'

'I'm sure you could have,' Lydia muttered sourly.

'Did you know that Sir Benedict intended to confront his niece and James Bromley at the temple that night?' John asked her bluntly.

'He wasn't likely to confide in me, was he?' she said scornfully. 'It's just the kind of thing he would do, though, now that I think on it.'

'So you were expecting something of the sort?'

'No. I only expected him to give Miss Portia a proper setdown.' She glanced from John to Lydia, realizing suddenly that she was under suspicion. 'I didn't know nothin', and I didn't do nothin' either. James killed Sir Ben, and he's goin' to hang for it. Serve him right, too!'

On these words, she stood up, looking at them defiantly. She was daring them to prove her wrong. Alas, they could not.

'Thank you, Bridget,' John said quietly. 'You have been most helpful.'

'You're welcome, I'm sure,' she said, her self-confidence restored.

'There is just one more thing,' he added.
'What is it?'

'Do you know whether anyone else but Jenkins was aware of your altercation with Sir Benedict?'

While she might not be familiar with a word like 'altercation', John's meaning was clear enough.

'I didn't see no one about, sir,' she answered slowly, as though straining to remember. 'I believe Mrs Leverett was asleep upstairs; Miss Padgett was reading to Mr Chetwin in the drawing-room down the hall; and of course Miss Portia was somewhere in the grounds, hiding from Sir Caleb.'

'I see.' John rose and nodded towards the door. 'That is all, Bridget.'

★   ★   ★

'Charming girl, Miss Pollard,' Lydia commented as soon as she was gone.

'Not the little innocent she appears with that golden hair and blue eyes,' he acknowledged.

'More like a budding barque of frailty, from what she has said today.'

'She will doubtless go far in her chosen . . . profession.'

'I begin to wonder whether I am in a

country house, or a bawdy house!'

Indeed, each person whom they interviewed produced a revelation of scandalous behaviour more fantastic than the last. Portia's affair with the stable hand was but the most blatant example — the one with whose particulars everyone was now acquainted. But what with Bridget raising her skirts to Sir Caleb at every opportunity, Miss Padgett offering a most unusual sort of 'consolation' to the blind, and Mrs Leverett expressing her gratitude to her late brother-in-law by sharing his bed whenever requested, Lydia was receiving a most comprehensive education in the intimate relations between men and women.

However interesting and informative this might be, it was not much help in solving the mystery of who had murdered Sir Benedict, always assuming, of course, that it was not James Bromley. At the moment, that young man's prospects did not seem at all propitious.

Lydia's last words had brought a smile to her husband's face, and he was just about to respond to them when he was forestalled in the most unfortunate manner. With lips parted and words at the ready, a piercing shriek prevented him from uttering more than one incomprehensible syllable.

The cry was clearly female, and was

followed by a series of muffled thumps which seemed to come from the general direction of the hallway. Now although Lydia had never actually heard the sound of a body falling down a flight of stairs, nor indeed witnessed such an event, the noises were so unmistakable that she could scarcely imagine any other explanation for them.

She leaped out of the chair in which she sat and bolted for the door. Whether she was more interested in observing what she did not doubt would be a most unpleasantly compelling sight, or in offering succour to the unfortunate victim, whomever it might be, she did not pause to consider. She knew only that she had no time to waste.

In the event, she collided with John's much more substantial frame just as she reached the door, almost incurring a serious accident herself. Her husband, however, managed to grab hold of her and prevent her from falling against the wall.

'Forgive me, Lydia!' he gasped, but she was too preoccupied to even note either his apology or the cause of it.

'Never mind that!' she cried. 'Someone is injured, John.'

'Pray God they are not dead.'

16

Upstairs and Down

Upon beholding the contorted heap of clothing and human flesh at the foot of the stairway, it looked as if John's prayers were in vain. It did not seem possible that the motionless form before them could yet harbour life within it. Lydia, never having been so near to a corpse before, instinctively halted rather than moving forward to examine what might well be the last mortal remains of . . . what appeared to be Miss Padgett.

For John, however, the experience was not quite so novel. He made three strides ahead, kneeling beside the poor woman. Before he could do more, however, another cry from the top of the stairs caused him to look up.

Lydia, also distracted by the piercing scream from above, raised her head in time to see Mrs Leverett collapse gracefully — an accomplishment which called forth a certain degree of reluctant admiration — on to the upper landing. After all, such a fine actress could hardly allow so dramatic a moment to go unchallenged, nor suffer herself to be outshone by a dead woman who was not even her social equal.

'You had better see to Mrs Leverett,' John said to Lydia, before bending once more over Miss Padgett.

Once again, however, he was interrupted in his task — this time by a gruff cry from behind.

'What is it?' Mr Chetwin demanded, emerging from the drawing-room and making his way along the hall towards the growing tumult. 'What has happened?'

His answer came from an unexpected source. Coming up behind him, Bridget spied John beside the prostrate Miss Padgett, and blurted out, 'Lawks, sir! Is poor Miss Padgett dead?'

'Dead!' Mr Chetwin cried. 'Delia! My God, has something happened to her?'

By now Lydia had brushed passed John and the fallen woman, but she turned at this heartfelt cry and looked back at Lawrence Chetwin. The fear and anguish upon his face made her pity him in that instance more than she had ever done since meeting him.

'She is hurt, yes,' John answered; and then, more comfortingly. 'But, fortunately, still alive.'

Lydia reached the landing and adjusted the long skirt of her own gown so that she might kneel beside Mrs Leverett. At this point they were joined by Portia, who had emerged from her bedchamber and traversed the upper hall to see what was going forward.

'Mama!' she exclaimed, looking down at her mother with Lydia beside her. Her face reflected as much annoyance as concern, Lydia thought.

'Fetch Mrs Leverett's hartshorn,' Lydia commanded, lifting the obscuring veil. There was no question that the lady would possess so necessary an accoutrement to feminine histrionics.

'But what of Delia — Miss Padgett?' Portia asked, peering over the banister at the much more interesting sight below.

'She is being attended to.'

Portia went away, and was back within seconds with the requested item, which Lydia passed under the pinched nostrils of the older woman. Immediately Mrs Leverett's head jerked slightly and her eyes opened to gaze in a bemused fashion at the two bending over her. There was no doubt that she was enjoying herself immensely. This was her moment, so to speak.

'Delia!' she moaned softly, allowing Lydia to support her shoulders as she mustered a fearful expression. 'Is she no more?'

'She is alive,' Lydia informed her, 'though in what condition I do not know.'

'Heaven be praised!' Mrs Leverett sat up and Lydia gladly relinquished her to the care of her daughter.

On the stairs beneath them, John had instructed Bridget to summon a doctor as quickly as she was able. The words were scarce out of his mouth when the front door was flung open and the figure of a man appeared in silhouette through the sunlight streaming into the aperture.

This newest addition to their gathering was none other than Cuthbert Kempton. He came forward and, seeing the dramatic tableau before him, offered any assistance which he might be able to render.

'Miss Padgett's gone and tumbled down the stairs, Mr Kempton,' Bridget informed him unnecessarily.

'Is she badly injured?'

'I do not know,' John said. 'Is there a doctor in town who can be brought here quickly?'

'Dr Bledsoe.' Kempton nodded. 'I will return directly and bring him back with me.'

'No.' John was his usual decisive self. 'If you have just ridden here, your horse will be too tired. Let one of the servants take a fresh mount and ride into town. You remain here and help me to get Miss Padgett to her bedchamber.'

'I'll tell Edgar to go at once.' Bridget was already halfway down the hall as she spoke.

'Very good.'

John had very gingerly managed to arrange Miss Padgett in a more decorous position, all the while feeling gently to see if there were any bones broken.

'I believe that her only real injury is to her head,' he pronounced now. 'She has been knocked completely insensible.'

'Should you like to try Mrs Leverett's *sal volatile*?'

Lydia was descending the stairs, the bottle in her hand, while Mr Kempton approached from the other side, ready to carry the poor woman upstairs again.

'Let us get her into bed first,' John said.

Between them, John and Mr Kempton lifted the governess from the stairs, John taking her upper body and the solicitor holding her legs. As carefully as possible, they carried her up, with Mrs Leverett lamenting over her and wringing her hands while Mr Chetwin followed in silence.

Having at last deposited her in her bed, propping her up with several pillows and placing a coverlet over her, John took the hartshorn from his wife and passed it before the lady's face.

Miss Padgett's reaction was not so quick or so marked as that of Mrs Leverett. She gave a low-toned grunt, but seemed still to be quite unconscious. A second attempt, however, produced more obvious benefits. Her eyelids raised, though only slightly, and she muttered something which sounded like, 'My head . . . my head.'

'Do you think we should even try to revive her?' Portia asked with belated concern.

By this time the lady's eyes had opened fully, though she seemed to have some difficulty in adjusting them to her surroundings. She closed them again, turning her head to one side and moaning.

'Do you know who I am, Miss Padgett?' John asked, with gentle firmness.

'You?' The eyes opened again. 'You are Mr . . . Mr Savidge.'

'I would say her senses are not impaired,' he announced to the rest. 'But it may be best to leave her be until the doctor arrives.'

'She is in a great deal of pain,' Lydia said, 'and someone should remain by her side.'

'I will sit with her.' Mr Chetwin was eager to offer his services.

'Surely a female would be a better nurse to

her,' Mr Kempton suggested, slightly scandalized.

'Oh, Winny will take good care of her,' Portia replied. 'He needs only to summon help if any is needed.'

So it was decided, and the rest of the party quit the room as hastily as possible.

* * *

Downstairs once more, they all gathered in the drawing-room to calm their nerves with some hot tea and inconsequential chatter. Portia thought that her mama might wish to return to her bed, but Mrs Leverett was strongly opposed to any such idea.

'I could not rest,' she insisted. 'How can anyone be at peace with such goings-on about them? My nerves are positively shattered.'

Besides which, Lydia thought to herself, in her bedchamber she would be deprived of a proper audience to witness her vapours and other evidences of her tender affection for the afflicted Miss Padgett — whom Mrs Leverett never thought of from one day to the next, she would wager, unless she required her for some errand or other.

'Poor Winny,' Portia said, more sincerely. 'He will be quite lost without her.'

'Nonsense!' her mother contradicted, not

wishing anyone to be thought worse off than herself. 'But for his reading, he scarcely needs Delia's help. I dare swear he can get about the estate without assistance from anyone. She is little more to him than a lapdog or a canary-bird.'

This last description was rather more *apropos* than she probably imagined, and Lydia had to stifle the urge to giggle. Only the remembrance that Miss Padgett's condition might be far more serious than they could tell at this point, kept her from disgracing herself.

'I could not believe my eyes,' Portia confessed, 'when I saw both you *and* Delia lying quite insensible — you at the top of the stairs and she at the bottom.'

'You were one of the first to arrive upon the scene, were you not, Mrs Leverett?' Lydia queried, seized by a sudden suspicion. Could the poor governess have been *pushed*? At least two members of the household had been upstairs. Either of them could have helped her down and then returned to their bedchamber and pretended to emerge from it.

'Indeed I was!' the lady declared grandly. 'So horrid a sight I never wish to behold again. And what with poor Benedict so lately having met such a gruesome end . . . ' Her voice trailed away with dramatic effect.

'Just so.'

'It certainly took *you* long enough to come to our aid,' Mrs Leverett turned upon her daughter accusingly. 'What with your own mother in peril, one would have thought that you would have wasted no time with primping in front of your glass!'

'I was *not* primping, Mama!' Portia objected strongly to this unjust description. 'Indeed, I had gone to lie down upon my bed, having slept little last night; and I thought the first cry I heard must have been a dream. Then, when I heard your own scream, I did indeed awaken and come to see what could be the matter.'

'Well, for a healthy young lady, you are precious slow to act, my dear, unless it be to beguile unsuitable young men.'

Mrs Leverett would not be pacified, and Lydia soon grew tired of the senseless bickering between the mother and daughter. Luckily, John provided a means of escape by turning to the prudently silent Mr Kempton and asking him if he would accompany him to the study to discuss a matter which had recently arisen.

The gentlemen were happy to escape, and Lydia immediately rose to join them. Portia looked at them suspiciously, but Mrs Leverett was enjoying herself too much at her daughter's expense to be overly concerned at their departure.

* * *

'What is it that you wish me to help you with, sir?' Mr Kempton asked, as soon as they entered the study.

Lydia sat down in the furthest chair, as had become her custom, to observe both men; while John took the seat behind the desk and motioned for the solicitor to follow his example.

'Let me be quite frank with you, Mr Kempton,' John stated without preamble, 'and inform you that we are quite aware that, in spite of your wife's assurances, you were not at home on the evening that Sir Benedict was murdered.'

Even Lydia was surprised at this unexpected gambit and, as for poor Mr Kempton, he was positively aghast. He looked as though he very much wanted to say something, but for a moment was quite deprived of any power to do so.

'How dare you, sir!' he cried at last, rising to his feet. Lydia wondered if he intended to flee, but he merely stood rooted to the spot before his chair. 'Of what are you accusing me?'

'Of nothing more than not being entirely honest with us,' John said smoothly. 'I have no proof of more than that . . . yet.'

'If you mean to accuse me of murdering Sir Benedict, you had best tell me why and how I should be supposed to have done so.'

'As to the how, I believe that is sufficiently understandable to anyone. Sir Benedict was shot with his own pistol, which you could easily have taken when you visited here earlier that afternoon.' John paused. 'The why, however, requires some explanation on my part.'

Without further roundaboutation, John related the particulars he had learned of Mr Kempton's quarrel with the late baronet. Hearing it so plainly spoken had a somewhat deflating effect upon the poor man, for he wilted back into his chair with all the fight apparently squeezed out of him.

'I admit that I had . . . borrowed money from Sir Benedict to pay certain debts.' A line of perspiration stood out on his brow, and he swallowed deep in his throat. 'I had hoped to . . . earn . . . an even greater sum which would have enabled me to repay him and to enlarge my own property. But it did not transpire the way I had anticipated.'

This sad tale, stripped of its useless prevarication, was easy enough for Lydia to decipher. The man had amassed gaming debts and, when Sir Benedict advanced him a sum of money to discharge them, he had foolishly gambled away even that amount in a vain attempt to win more money. It was a common enough story, which was sadly comic in its way.

'So you admit that you had good cause to kill Sir Benedict?'

'Never!' Mr Kempton had been gazing down at the hands which he kept folded in his lap. At this, however, he looked up with desperate resolution. 'I would never have done such a thing, sir, whatever you may believe. Nor can you prove differently. I fully intended to sell my horse, Wanderer, and pay back every penny of the money which I owed.'

John gave him a considering look, and he returned it resolutely.

'You did not anticipate that Sir Benedict might dispense with your services . . . might expose you to censure and contempt among your acquaintance, at least?'

'No sir.' Kempton shook his head in firm denial, adding with something of a sneer, 'He was much more concerned that his neighbours not know that *I* had made a fool of *him*. His own pride would not have allowed him to expose me, for the sake of being laughed at.'

'And where,' John continued, 'were you on

the night that Sir Benedict died?'

'I was at a spot some three miles distant from Fallowfield.' He coughed delicately, shooting an embarrassed glance at Lydia. 'I would not wish to say what kind of establishment it might be in front of a lady.'

'Were you at a bawdy-house?' Lydia demanded, her mind reverting to the one form of amusement to which everyone at Fallowfield seemed peculiarly attached.

Mr Kempton was clearly shocked at her bald indelicacy. No doubt he considered her a woman of low breeding and no sensibility. Well, she supposed he was not so very wrong. She was not of the gentry, but then, neither was he. And as for the fine feelings which would have prevented her from speaking what she thought, they meant little to her since they were not usually genuine.

'Madam,' he said austerely, 'I have never frequented such establishments.'

'Your wife would not permit it, I suppose.' Only after she said the words did she realize that she had spoken aloud. The look of disgust on the gentleman's face told her that she had sunk beneath reproach in his eyes.

'I was attending a cockfight on the night to which you are referring.'

Privately, Lydia did not consider this a great improvement over her own conjecture.

On the contrary, it indicated that he was still inclined to throw his money away on a form of gaming which was particularly distasteful and even cruel. She would almost have thought better of him had he been seeking the charms of some country trollop.

'And you never came near Fallowfield?' John pressed the issue, determined to get to the truth.

'Not closer than a mile, sir. I swear it on my honour.'

★ ★ ★

They returned to the drawing-room several minutes later. All was calm, the two combatants having apparently declared a truce. Nothing of any moment was said for full fifteen minutes, and Lydia was almost ready to nod off into a comfortable doze when the sound of some slight commotion at the front entrance denoted the arrival of Doctor Bledsoe.

The good doctor was a somewhat rugged, pock-marked gentleman who nevertheless seemed kind enough. While the others waited below, he was shown up to Miss Padgett's chamber by Jenkins, and returned in a very short space of time. His observations were brief and not much more than they knew already. Miss Padgett had fallen down the stairs and suffered a blow to her head. She must be watched carefully for a day or two, for signs of any lingering malady to the brain, but otherwise there was not much to be done. He had given her a concoction of his own making for the pain in her head and her limbs, which were considerably bruised but had miraculously escaped being broken.

'She is a most fortunate lady,' he said in his gruff way.

He told them that if he was needed he might be summoned at any hour, and would have departed at once, had not Mrs Leverett detained him with a catalogue of her own aches and complaints which kept him occupied for quite half an hour. Indeed, she would not release him from her clutches until she had persuaded him that she was in desperate need of a sedative draught. Once this had been administered, she was perfectly content and went up to her bed in excellent spirits.

Mr Kempton, having assured himself that Miss Padgett was in no immediate danger, was in no mood to remain at Fallowfield, and excused himself with almost indecent haste. Even Portia deserted them, claiming that she was quite exhausted herself, and went up to her bedchamber.

'What shall we do now, John?'

'Would you object to a walk while the sun is still up?'

'I do not think that I would object to anything which got me out of this house.'

17

Miss Padgett Speaks

Considering the events which had already occurred, the day was not very far advanced and they had ample time to stroll about the grounds — which were quite lovely even with most of the trees almost stripped naked of their leaves.

The park was large enough for them to enjoy a variety of scenes as they discussed the progress of their enquiries thus far.

'Do you begin to see your way clearly, John?' Lydia asked.

John confessed that although there were many tantalizing hints as to what might have occurred here more than a sennight before, nothing as yet seemed to make any sense.

'Everyone,' Lydia pointed out, 'had a reason for killing Sir Benedict.'

'And no one,' he added, kicking a stray leaf out of their path, 'can prove to us where they were when the deed was done.'

'I have said it before, but it still amazes me,

when one considers that almost no one in this house slept in their own bed, and yet on that night each of them was, apparently, quite alone.'

'And what do you think of this latest development?'

'Mr Kempton's excuse that he was at a cockfight?'

'I was referring to Miss Padgett's fall,' he corrected her. 'Although, if what Kempton says is true, it may eliminate him as a suspect.'

'Not necessarily.' She shook her head. 'Even if he did attend the cockfight, he might have slipped away for a time in order to commit the crime.'

John considered the matter, but decided that it was unlikely. There would not have been so very many men there that they would not notice if one of them were missing.

'Even if they were intent on the cocks, rather than on each other?' Lydia was sceptical.

'It would not be difficult to ascertain the names of some of those present in order to verify his story.'

'But might he not be able to pay for them to support him in his tale?'

'Bribery?' He chuckled. 'It seems that our good Mr Kempton has not a feather to fly with.'

'Blown up at *point non plus*,' she agreed. 'But still it is not proof of his innocence.'

'Nor of his guilt,' he reminded her. 'It will take much more than such conjectures to convince the local authorities that James Bromley is not their man.'

'Being a stable hand, he is so much more suitable a felon, I suppose.'

'Precisely what I was thinking.'

Lydia pondered this for a moment, watching a squirrel scamper away beyond a hedgerow with some seed to store away for the approaching winter. It seemed quite hopeless. Nothing they had learned appeared to be of the slightest use.

'Do you think,' she said, returning to his original question, 'that Miss Padgett's fall was a mere accident?'

'I intend to ask her at the earliest opportunity,' he admitted.

'If you ask me,' Lydia said unhopefully, 'she is just the sort of woman who would trip over her own shadow.'

'Undoubtedly she is. But did she do so on this occasion?'

'Why would anyone push her down the stairs?'

'Something she had seen, perhaps . . .'

'It might be something which she did not understand, but which might later strike her as odd.'

'I find it all very hard to believe,' he confessed.

Lydia sighed. They had circumnavigated the lake shore and arrived back at the Temple of the Seven Virtues. This was where it had all begun. Here the two young lovers would meet for midnight trysts, and here Sir Benedict had come to put an end to their affair. Instead, someone else had put an end to *him*.

'But if it is so, then the poor woman is in great danger. Whoever tried to kill her has not succeeded, and is not likely to be content to leave his or her job undone.'

'Then there is no time to be lost, is there?'

Whether it was this thought which spurred them to quicken their pace, or the sudden realization that if they tarried much longer they would be late for supper, it was certainly true that they made their way back from the temple in far less time than it had taken them to arrive there.

Their evening ablutions were accomplished with almost indecent haste, and it was with a distinct feeling of accomplishment that they presented themselves in the drawing-room a full quarter of an hour before they were to dine.

★   ★   ★

As they entered the room, Lydia could not help but think what a pretty scene of domestic tranquillity it presented. There was Portia seated on the sofa, reading from a volume of Byron's poetry. Mr Chetwin was nodding off in a chair by a roaring fire which dispelled the chill which had descended after sunset. To complete the picture, Mrs Leverett was positioned on the other side of the fireplace, bent over a tambour frame on which she was carefully completing an intricate and quite useless piece of embroidery. Not that anyone had ever heard of a *useful* piece of embroidery, Lydia reflected. Needlework, like virtue, must be its own reward.

A casual observer would scarcely credit that this house had just been the scene of a terrible crime and an accident which might or might not be quite so innocent as it seemed. The trio before them was so stolid and respectable that Lydia had to force herself to remember that each of them had been conducting clandestine affairs under this very roof for some time.

After the first polite greetings were past and Mr Chetwin had roused himself from peaceful repose, John enquired after Miss Padgett.

'She is feeling much more the thing,' the

other man reassured him, but could not resist fanning the flame a little. 'In my opinion, it is all the hubbub of your questions and useless enquiries which unsettled her so that she became inattentive and lost her footing on the stairs.'

'Was it?' John asked, not in the least perturbed. 'Do you not think that it might have been concern that there is a murderer loose among us?'

'The man responsible for Sir Benedict's death is in gaol, sir.'

'Are you certain of that?'

'I know it almost as surely as if . . . as if I had seen him do the deed myself!'

'I will not have you utter such slanders in my presence, Winny!' Portia immediately flew to the defence of her beloved. 'James is no more guilty of my uncle's death than I am.'

'Well said, my fine miss!' Mr Chetwin's sneer was worthy of a better audience than this, Lydia considered. His scorn was positively magnificent. 'You and that servant between you are the cause of all our sorrows.'

'Please!' Mrs Leverett finally chose to speak her lines, recognizing belatedly that she was being denied the principal role in this drama. 'You run roughshod over my nerves, the pair of you. Must I be subjected to this brangling, after the horrors of this day — I who have already lost my dearest friend and brother-in-law?'

This was an opportunity which Mr Chetwin could not resist.

'I admire your restraint, my dear Pamela,' he said viciously. 'I, of all people, know that Benedict was far more to you than that!'

'What do you mean, Winny?' Portia demanded, letting Byron fall unheeded to the ground.

'He means to be facetious, I suppose,' Mrs Leverett said quickly. 'But we are not amused by your jests, Lawrence.'

'I didn't think you would be.'

Portia, however, had been quick to grasp his meaning. With her newfound knowledge of her mother's less than respectable past, it required no great leap of imagination for her to comprehend that Mrs Leverett's long-ago connection with her brother-in-law might not have been as far in the past as she would have wished.

'You do not mean to say,' she cried, addressing herself to her mama, 'that you and Uncle Benedict still . . . that you were . . . after all this time . . . ?'

'I do not mean to say anything at all,' the much harassed mother said defensively. 'I am not on trial here, am I?'

'I cannot believe it!' Yet it seemed that Miss

Leverett *did* believe it, for she followed with, 'I am appalled by your conduct, Mama! How could you do such a thing?'

'A fine one you are to be censuring my behaviour, miss!'

She drew a deep breath, about to launch into a fine speech which, Lydia had no doubt, would have rivalled anything in Shakespeare. Unfortunately, before she could continue, the clock on the mantel chimed the hour, and she was recalled to a sense of her duties. Instead of ringing a peal over her daughter, therefore, she descended at once from the sublimely comic to the tragically mundane, announcing blandly, 'It is time for us to go in to supper.'

So much, Lydia thought, for the domestic tranquillity of English country life.

★ ★ ★

Supper began in almost complete silence, but for the occasional innocuous remark from Lydia or John. Portia spent the time glowering at her mother, who affected to ignore her; Mr Chetwin was lost in a brown study, for which Lydia could not, in all conscience, blame him.

The entrances and exits of the servants

with the various courses provided some relief from this curious monotony. The silence was broken at length by John.

'You will be glad to hear, Mrs Leverett,' he said, 'that my wife and I shall be leaving you tomorrow.'

Portia immediately removed her gimlet stare from the direction of her mama and looked directly at him.

'You cannot leave yet!' she cried, almost frantic. 'You have not discovered who killed my uncle.'

'As if we do not know,' Mr Chetwin murmured.

'We promised you only three days,' John reminded the young lady. 'That was our bargain, whether we were able to find the truth or not. Tomorrow makes the third day, and we shall be gone by noon.'

'It is quite hopeless, then,' Portia cried, sinking at once into despair.

'We are not gone yet,' Lydia reminded her, though privately she was convinced that they had failed. She also had to own that she did not like the flavour of defeat. It was far too bitter.

When they had finished their meal some time later, the Savidges excused themselves at once and made their way up to their bedchamber. On their way, they paused beside the door to Miss Padgett's room.

'Shall we look in on her?' Lydia whispered doubtfully.

'If she is asleep, we will not disturb her,' John cautioned, very gingerly turning the handle and pushing inward.

★ ★ ★

They peered into the semi-gloom to find Delia Padgett sitting up in bed. Her eyes were darkly shadowed, looking positively skeletal in her peaked white face. Lydia thought that she had never seen a sadder-looking visage in all her life. She was awake, at least. It seemed almost heartless to be questioning her at such a time, after her recent ordeal, but Lydia knew that it was unlikely they would have another opportunity to do so.

'How are you feeling, ma'am?' Lydia asked softly, going up to the foot of the bed and staring down at the lonely little figure lying there.

'I — I am well enough, thank God,' she said, her eyes turning to focus on John, who stood behind his wife.

'Dr Bledsoe seems to think that you will be quite your old self with but a few days' rest, Miss Padgett.'

'Perhaps so, Mr Savidge.' She did not

sound very hopeful.

'Can you tell us what happened, ma'am?'

She looked up at that, her eyes narrowed in sudden fear.

'Why do you want to know?'

'Someone was killed here only days ago.' John was unusually solemn and severe.

'What has that to do with me?' She looked as though she would have jumped up from the bed and fled the room, but had not the strength.

'Perhaps nothing at all.' He smiled encouragingly. 'If you say that your fall was merely an accident, then I suppose we need not say any more.'

'Of course it was an accident. What else could it be?'

'Tell me, Miss Padgett,' he continued, 'did you overhear an argument which Sir Benedict had on the day of his death?'

She looked absolutely horrified. Lydia was afraid that her nerves would not bear the strain, and almost signalled to John to desist.

'Did you hear such an argument?' he repeated.

'I . . . well, I *did* hear voices raised in the hall at one time,' she admitted. 'I would not say that it was an argument, precisely, but surely a very — animated — discussion.'

'And one of the persons involved in this

discussion was Sir Benedict?'

'I *thought* I heard his voice.' She caught her lips between her teeth. 'I might have been mistaken, though, might I not?'

It seemed she was very eager for someone to tell her that she had been in error. Neither of the two before her, however, could oblige.

'Where were you at the time?' Lydia inquired.

'In — in the drawing-room.'

'With Mr Chetwin?'

She hesitated a moment. 'Y-yes. I was reading to him from *Tristram Shandy*, an old favourite of his, you know.'

'Indeed.' John smiled in a vain attempt to put her at her ease. 'With whom was Sir Benedict arguing?'

'Really, I could not be sure.' She licked her lips, which prompted Lydia to ask if she required some water. Miss Padgett refused.

'You have no idea who the other person might have been?'

'It was very faint,' she said more confidently. 'I thought it was — it might have been Bridget, one of the maids. It would not have been the first time that she had given cause for reproof.'

'Do you know the cause of the argument — if argument it was?'

'I cannot say, sir.' She looked him directly

in the eye to emphasize her point. 'They were too great a distance from the drawing-room. It was impossible for me to hear what they were speaking of. I assure you, I heard nothing.'

Since she was so insistent on this point, it was useless to press her further.

'And nothing else about that day occurs to you as being odd or of particular note?'

'Nothing.'

'Your fall this morning — ' he began, but could get no further before she interrupted him.

'If you mean to imply that I was pushed, sir, the suggestion is ludicrous! Why would anyone do such a thing?'

'If you knew something about Sir Benedict's murder — '

Once again she refused to let him finish his sentence.

'I know nothing . . . nothing, I tell you! I saw nothing!' She was almost hysterical now. 'I tripped on my train, or — or something. I tripped. That is all.'

'You are quite sure?' he persisted.

'Quite sure.' Now she did break into tears, beginning to sob uncontrollably. 'Why must you keep asking me these things? Nobody in this house would ever harm me, Mr Savidge. Nobody, I tell you!'

'There, there, Miss Padgett.' Lydia went to her side, pushing her gently back against the pillows, from which she had risen in her sudden passion. 'Of course they would not.'

'Nobody would want to kill me,' she said more calmly, though the tears continued to flow from her eyes. 'Nobody in this house is so cold and cruel as to harm me . . . or Sir Benedict either. It was all a mistake . . . a terrible, terrible mistake. It must have been . . . surely it must have been.'

'Of course it was,' Lydia hastened to reassure her. 'But you must try to rest, ma'am. We will leave you now, and all will be well, I am certain of it.'

'Why did you have to come here?' she asked, though it seemed to Lydia that she was speaking more to herself than to them. 'If only you had not come here.'

'We will be leaving tomorrow, Miss Padgett.'

'You will?' The older woman looked up hopefully. 'Are you quite certain of that?'

'Quite.'

She sighed, as if relieved. Lydia knew not whether to laugh or to be annoyed with her. Nobody could have been so eager to see the last of someone as she seemed to be at the prospect of their departure. Surely she must know something!

Before she could say more, however, they were joined by Miss Leverett, all solicitude for her former governess. For the next few minutes, nothing but polite platitudes were exchanged, and then the other three quit the room.

★ ★ ★

'Poor Delia!' Portia exclaimed as soon as they had closed the door behind them. 'She is very poorly tonight.'

'Hardly surprising, I would say.'

'Of course, Mr Savidge.' Then, brightening, she added, 'But I have charged Winny to come up and sit with her awhile. That will be as good as a tonic to her, I do not doubt. She has always had a bit of a *tendre* for him, of course. Mama and I have quizzed her about it for years.'

'Miss Padgett and Mr Chetwin?' Lydia's pretended surprise was as well acted as anything Mrs Leverett could achieve in that line.

'Oh yes.' Portia laughed outright. 'I daresay it is no wonder. Delia was never a beauty, and when Winny started paying her attention — having no other eligible female at hand — it is no wonder if her poor head was turned. I thought at one time they might

198

marry. But Winny probably thinks her beneath his touch. Although he is not related to us by blood, he thinks of himself as quite one of the Stanbury family, and Delia is a mere vicar's daughter.'

'Only a fool would let that prevent him from offering for a lady, if he cared for her.'

'Winny is a very proud man, even more so than Uncle Benedict, if that were possible.'

'I am very sorry, Miss Leverett,' John said now, turning the subject, 'that we have been of so little help to you. It seems that we have failed in our efforts on your behalf.'

'You have abandoned hope, then?'

'I would not go so far as to say that,' he admitted. 'But we have come to the point where we are unable to make sense of what we have learned thus far.'

'We still have until tomorrow morning,' Lydia said irrepressibly. After all, she could not bear to think of quitting when a man's life hung in the balance. They had saved a man from the gallows before. Had it been mere luck, or could they have a gift for such things?

'You are still confident of success?' John smiled in spite of himself as he looked down at his wife.

'Not precisely confident.' She sighed. 'It does not appear very auspicious at the moment. But I am not ready to surrender quite so easily.'

'Well,' Portia said, with a look of grim determination on her face, 'if you are unable to solve this riddle, I will be forced to take matters into my own hands.'

18

Plans and Puzzles

'What do you mean, Miss Leverett?' Lydia asked, intrigued by her cryptic remark. 'What have you in mind?'

'Nothing too desperate, I trust?' John seemed to harbour some misgiving.

'I cannot allow the father of my child to be hanged like a common criminal,' Portia said reasonably.

Lydia only just managed to refrain from commenting that, were he to be found guilty and hanged for murder, he *would* be a common criminal — at least in the eyes of His Majesty's Government and the surrounding populace. Instead, she schooled her features into a semblance of calm and agreed with the girl that such a fate must be prevented at all costs.

'But how do you mean to prevent it?'

'I have not determined all the details of a plan as yet, but I must free him from prison, at all events.'

'A laudable ambition.' Lydia began to enter into the spirit of her quest. 'But I think you should lose no time in working out how it is to be accomplished. One must leave nothing to chance in such cases.'

'What would you do, Lydia?' Miss Leverett expressed a flattering reliance upon the talents of her new acquaintance.

'First,' Lydia said, 'one must discover how many are guarding the prisoner.'

'There are mostly two men in attendance. Occasionally a third may be present.'

'You are positive of this?'

'Oh yes.' Portia nodded decisively. 'I have been there on several occasions myself, as I told you before.'

'Then nothing could be easier.'

'Nothing at all,' John concurred, his eyes twinkling appreciatively at his wife's aplomb.

'Might my uncle's pistol be of use, do you think?' Portia asked.

'Quite unnecessary, my dear girl.'

'One would not wish to make too much noise.' John raised a finger to emphasize his point. 'It might frighten the children living nearby.'

'I had not thought of that.' Portia was quite unconscious of satire.

'This is what I would advise,' Lydia

pronounced so seriously that Portia was quite taken in.

Her plan was crude, but might well be effective if one were thick-skulled enough to attempt it. The next time Dr Bledsoe was called to attend to Miss Padgett, Portia was to purloin some of the sedative draught which he prescribed. This was to be introduced into a bottle of wine from her late uncle's cellar. Portia might then call upon James, and offer the wine to his gaolers as a token of her appreciation for their kind treatment of the accused.

'I do not think,' Portia said, 'that they are permitted to drink wine while guarding their prisoner.'

'No doubt they are not *supposed* to do so,' Lydia remarked sapiently. 'That does not say, however, that they will refrain from doing so once nobody is about to observe them.'

Portia agreed that this might well be so.

'And,' Lydia said in conclusion, 'once they have swallowed the concoction, you may slip back into the gaol. They will be lying insensible upon the floor.'

'Or slumped over a table, perhaps,' John suggested.

'Perhaps.' She allowed him this possible variation upon her theme. 'Either way, Portia can easily take the keys, release James, and the two of them can fly into the night.'

'Whither shall they fly, my dear wife?' John asked, ever practical.

'*That*,' she answered grandly, 'is something which we must consider next.'

'Oh.'

'There can be no question what we must do after that,' Portia told them, her eyes glowing at the thought of such a dangerous adventure. 'We shall make our way to the coast and take a ship sailing for America!'

'There should be no difficulty in *that*,' John admitted, and Lydia could see that he found it difficult to stifle his laughter.

'None at all,' she replied. 'All is settled, then.'

'Indeed.' Portia actually embraced her in her enthusiasm for the crack-brained scheme. 'You may not have been able to clear James's name, but you have shown me how I can save his life. I do thank you so much, my dear Lydia.'

'I am happy to oblige in any way I can.'

'I must take great care when Dr Bledsoe comes again.'

'In the meantime,' John ventured to say, 'I think we had all better retire for the night. We shall need our rest if we are to travel tomorrow. And you must conserve your strength for your more momentous enterprise, Miss Leverett.'

With further protestations of thanks, Portia flitted away to her bedchamber, while the others made their way down the hallway to theirs.

★ ★ ★

'You are a most wicked young lady, my dear,' John informed his wife when they had gained the privacy of their room.

'I do not know when I have enjoyed anything half as much!' she confessed, giving way to her merriment at last.

'She means to carry out your plan, you know.'

'Of course she does.' Lydia was quite indignant. 'It is an excellent one, is it not? And I'll wager she carries it off in grand style too.'

'I hope it will not come to that.'

'Well, John, we are — to borrow an apt phrase — her *last best hope*.'

'Heaven help her!'

'Help me unclasp my necklace.'

Lydia turned her back to him and inclined her head while he performed this office. Then she removed her slippers and lay down upon the bed, giving no thought to the condition of her second-best gown, which she did not bother to change. A moment later, John tossed aside his own footwear and heaved himself on to the bed beside her. For a newlywed couple, however, they displayed remarkably little interest in each other. Instead, they lay side by side, staring up at the ceiling in mutual concentration.

'We have mere hours in which to solve this riddle we have been set,' John said to the plaster above.

'I fear it will be a long night.'

'Let us review everything which we have learned thus far. Surely we can find the truth in the midst of it all.'

Still looking above, Lydia consented.

'First,' John began slowly, 'we must decide who had good reason to kill Sir Benedict.'

'Cuthbert Kempton springs immediately to mind,' Lydia answered drily. 'He stood to lose everything if Sir Benedict demanded that his loan be repaid.'

'But would Sir Benedict have done so?'

'It seems a reasonable enough request.'

'But somehow I do not think that he would have pressed the matter if Mr Kempton were to promise to return the money in due time.'

Lydia did remove her gaze from the ceiling at this, turning her head to regard her husband with some curiosity.

'The gentleman seems to have been something of a tyrant,' she reminded him.

'With the exception of Mr Chetwin, nobody was exactly fond of him.'

'What of Mrs Leverett?' he countered mischievously.

'No doubt she enjoyed the occasional romp in his bed.' Lydia did not mince her words. 'But in spite of her exaggerated mourning, I think her feelings are not particularly strong for anyone but herself.'

'*L'amour de soi*,' John murmured. 'Yes, you are right. She preferred him to her husband as a lover. But they shared only pleasure, without any degree of real attachment.'

'No doubt she was as fond of him as her nature would allow. But while she will make a great parade of grief, she is not likely to go into a decline.'

She might, they considered, have learned of his plan to disinherit her daughter, and sought to stop him before he could bring it to fruition. But how would she have known that he would be going to the temple that evening? Besides which, as Lydia pointed out, she did not seem to be conversant with guns, and was not the sort of woman who was likely to employ such crude and messy means.

'Poison would be her weapon of choice, if one can consider poison to be a weapon at all,' she said.

'But once again I return to Sir Benedict.' John looked at Lydia, shaking his head. 'Like many a hound, my impression is that his bark was far more ferocious than his bite was like to be.'

'How so?'

'Miss Leverett has given us the impression that he was tyrannical, as you say.'

'Indeed.'

'But although he tried to persuade her to marry the so unsuitable Sir Caleb, it does not seem that he ever seriously tried to *force* the match on her.'

'True.' Lydia thought the matter over, deciding that John might have the right of it. 'Portia seems to have started her affair with James Bromley partly out of wilful spite, and partly due to the dearth of good-looking men of her own station in the neighbourhood.'

John turned on his side, positioning himself with his elbow. 'Also, Sir Benedict was eager enough to invite his former sweetheart to live at Fallowfield and make her daughter his heiress.'

'But he was at least partially convinced that she was his own daughter.'

'Yes, but consider how easily he was persuaded of that fact! And,' John continued, 'I do not believe that he ever had the least intention of cutting Miss Leverett out of his will.'

'Why go to the trouble of making a new will, then?' Lydia asked reasonably.

'I think he meant merely to use it to bring the girl to her senses, as he saw it.' John's eyes squinted, as though looking back into the past, and into the late Sir Benedict's mind. 'It was to be a threat, but one I am convinced he had no intention of carrying out.'

'Sir Benedict becomes a man of bluster, but not one of action . . . ' Lydia followed his thought, though it brought them no closer to a solution.

'He did not even dismiss Bridget for her conduct, which he could easily have done on the spot.'

'Which is very much the way he dealt with Mr Kempton on the same day.'

'They might have all cordially disliked him, but I think each knew that they were in no real danger from him.'

'But then,' Lydia cried in some exasperation, 'you are saying that *nobody* wanted to kill the man!'

'Obviously someone did.'

'Mr Kempton remains the most likely suspect.'

Lydia enumerated the reasons for her statement. First, Mr Kempton had quarrelled with the deceased on the day of his murder. Perhaps there had been more to the quarrel than the gardener had heard. Secondly, Mr Kempton and his wife had both lied about his whereabouts that night. And finally, from what they had learned, it seemed that he would have had ample opportunity to ride over from the cockfight he claimed to have attended, and shot Sir Benedict.

'But why,' John demanded, 'should he have gone to the trouble of first coming into the house — where he ran the risk of being discovered by someone — in order to don his victim's coat? It makes no sense at all, Lydia.'

'Let us consider.' Lydia took the whip to her imagination and tooled it around her mind for a moment. 'He went in to steal the pistol — '

'Which he could have easily taken from the room after their argument earlier that day,' John interrupted, crushingly.

'And he grabbed the coat from its hook as he passed on his way to the kitchen door,' she finished, preferring to ignore his remark.

'It will not do,' John insisted. 'Only consider that he could far more easily have gone directly to the temple, and either strangled or stabbed Sir Benedict without putting himself to all the trouble you have described.'

'And there is one thing which I cannot account for,' she confessed grudgingly.

'Which is?' He smiled at her crestfallen look.

'How did he know that Sir Benedict would be at the temple that night?'

'That remains the greatest mystery of all,' John admitted. 'It seems the only one who might have guessed his intention was Bridget, the maid.'

'I can easily imagine *her* in the role of a murderess!'

'So can I.'

In fact, the two people who seemed ruthless enough to have done such a deed were both women: Bridget and Miss Leverett herself. Portia certainly had a great deal to lose if she were disinherited, but it was unlikely that she was aware that such a fate might befall her. She had told them, however, that she was a fine shot, having been taught by her uncle himself. She had the skill required, and she had the motive, but as far as they could tell, she was as ignorant as anyone of her uncle's intentions.

As for Bridget, even if she had some idea of what Sir Benedict's reaction might be when she exposed to him his niece's clandestine affair, she could not have been certain that he would be confronting the guilty pair that very evening. Also, it would be difficult to prove that she knew anything of pistols, though it was a possibility.

'In addition to all this,' John concluded, 'I am convinced that she was not really afraid of Sir Benedict. The very fact that she had the temerity to throw Portia's affair in his face shows that she was not intimidated by his threats.'

Lydia sank back into her pillows, quite discouraged. Round and round they went, but always returned to the place they began.

'But that leaves us with only Mr Chetwin and Miss Padgett,' she said.

'And what motive could either of them have had to kill Sir Benedict?'

Lydia sighed deeply. 'Mr Chetwin seems to have had none at all. He was Sir Benedict's only true friend, and had been so since his childhood. Even you cannot deny that his sorrow over this is perhaps the only genuine emotion we have encountered since we came here.'

'Except for Miss Padgett's this evening,' he admitted. 'She is the most timid and retiring of our suspects — the one I would be inclined to be least suspicious of. And yet I have the distinct impression that she knows more than she is telling us.'

'Could she possibly have killed Sir Benedict, in the hope that Mr Chetwin would inherit the estate, and that she might become mistress of Fallowfield, as she was of its new master?'

John, however, would have none of it. He pointed out two serious flaws in this flight of fancy: Firstly, Miss Padgett had no reason to believe that Mr Chetwin was more likely to marry her after inheriting the estate than he had been before. Most damaging to this theory, though, was the simple fact that the will in question had not been signed. By killing Sir Benedict before he could make the document official, Miss Padgett would have effectively prevented Lawrence Chetwin from ever inheriting Fallowfield.

'In fact,' he said in conclusion, 'she would have had every reason in the world to keep the man alive until the will was signed and witnessed.'

'Perhaps,' Lydia said desperately, 'she has no understanding of legal matters.'

'The woman may be a mouse,' her husband said unflatteringly, 'and given to nerves and vapours, but I'd wager she is no fool.'

'So now,' Lydia announced grandly, 'we have eliminated every single suspect, and must conclude that Sir Benedict was murdered by the Ghost of Fallowfield, or some such thing!'

'Not at all.' John was quite unruffled. 'You are forgetting one thing which all these people have in common.'

'What is that?'

'None of them has anyone who can verify where they were at the time Sir Benedict was killed.'

'Well . . . ' Lydia thought about it. 'Portia has James Bromley.'

'No.' John rolled on to his back again and crossed his arms. 'James and Portia were supposedly on the same path in the park, but neither saw the other until they met over the body of the victim.'

'Oh.'

'Portia could have killed Sir Benedict and stood over the body until James arrived, pretending to have just discovered it.'

'Or,' Lydia put forward, 'James might have killed Sir Benedict, gone out of the temple and hidden behind a convenient hedge until Portia ran up to the door. He could then have emerged and acted as though he had run up behind her.'

'Similarly, any member of the household *could* conceivably have taken the pistol, stolen out of the house in the darkness, and done the deed without anyone ever knowing, as you and I proved last night.'

Lydia now sat up, frowning at him.

'But this only makes everything more difficult. Everyone had the opportunity to kill the poor man, yet nobody had sufficient reason to do so.'

'And there you have it.'

'Have what?' she cried.

'Our dilemma.'

She was strongly tempted to box his ears. What was the use of pointing out what had been obvious almost from the beginning? The fact was, they were not a whit nearer to their goal.

'It seems to me that the key to the puzzle,' she said after some struggle with herself, 'is the bloodstained greatcoat.'

'If the stains upon it are indeed blood.'

'It was *you* who first suggested as much.'

'It is possible that I was wrong.'

Lydia groaned. 'You give me the headache, John.'

'I do not believe that I am wrong, however.'

'You might as well be,' she said severely. 'For the coat makes less sense than anything. Why would anyone do something so odd, so foolish?'

'It seems an impossible conundrum.'

'But there *must* be an answer.'

John could not deny this. On the other hand, when he asked her what the answer might be, her response was to give him a sharp pinch upon the arm and call him a great gudgeon. Of course there was an answer, and there was something they had missed which must reveal it. Since they *had* missed it, however, it was useless to quiz her so. She longed more than ever for her papa. He had been such a great help to them — albeit unwittingly — in sniffing out a killer. That had all hinged on the words of a maid, and a chance remark spoken in jest. If only it might prove as simple in this instance.

For more than an hour afterward they debated and discussed all they could recall from the past two days. Each conversation was turned upside down and inside out, but to no avail. They remained mired in the muck of their own endless conjectures, the wheels of their minds endlessly turning without going anywhere.

'There seems nothing for it,' Lydia said at last, 'but to pray for guidance.'

'Do you think it will serve?'

'Surely nothing but the intervention of Divine Providence can avail us at this point.'

'Well, we had better make our petitions and go to sleep.'

'Sleep!' Lydia gave a most unfeminine snort of disgust. 'I am not like to sleep tonight.'

'In that case,' John said, levering himself closer and beginning to nuzzle her throat, 'we had better think of some way to pass the time until morning.'

'John!' She could not repress a *frisson* of pleasure at the all too enjoyable sensation invoked by his lips on her bare skin. 'You are abominable. How can you think of such a thing at a time like this?'

'Because I am a man,' he said simply. 'And, moreover, a man who has only recently married and is not yet inured to the charms of his young bride.'

'You are too romantic, sir,' she protested, locking her arms around his neck.

Ah well! Perhaps John was right. If one must stay awake, one might as well enjoy it.

★ ★ ★

It was some time later that Lydia looked down at her husband, who was sleeping like a newborn babe. How like a man! Once his desires were satisfied, all was well with his world. Unfortunately for her, she was a woman. She could not help but dwell on everything that had transpired since they came to Fallowfield. But nothing which either reason or imagination could produce in her mind had any result but ever-increasing frustration.

Who killed Sir Benedict Stanbury? The

question echoed over and over, but the only answer was silence. Was not silence itself a virtue? If only the walls of the Temple of the Seven Virtues could speak. What secrets they could tell. Dark secrets . . . as dark and cold as the grave where Sir Benedict's body lay. Could Sir Benedict ever be truly at rest while his death remained unavenged and his killer was allowed to go free? And perhaps more to the point, as far as Lydia was concerned, could *she*?

19

Divine Providence

The next morning, Lydia crawled out of bed with a throbbing head and bruised-looking eyes. She could not have felt more completely crushed, she reflected, if the Prince Regent himself had been seated upon her the whole night long — accompanied by his feckless brothers, the six disgraceful Royal Dukes. It was no wonder, she thought inconsequently, that poor King George had gone mad, with such unpropitious offspring to follow after him.

She took her time getting dressed, hardly noticing John, who was similarly taciturn — though much more well-rested, the brute! They made their way downstairs to breakfast, which they consumed in total silence. Neither of them wished to speak. In truth, she supposed they did not know what to say to each other.

She could hardly believe that they had failed so abjectly. When they accepted Miss

Leverett's proposition, it had been with light hearts and high hopes. The possibility that they might not accomplish their task had been so remote, at least to Lydia's mind, that it was unworthy of serious consideration. Now here they sat, eating food which tasted like sand, and still racking their brains to discern some faint glimmer of light amidst the encroaching darkness.

It was not so much a matter of their own pride, but when she thought of the probable fate of James Bromley, she felt quite ill and let her spoon fall with a loud clatter.

'Perhaps we did not make our petition humbly enough,' John remarked with a feeble attempt at humour. Even his imperturbable spirits were not proof against the gloom.

'Oh John — '

'Your carriage is being brought round now, sir.'

This last was spoken by Jenkins, who appeared as if by magic from the nether regions of the house. But for a few maids who had dropped respectful curtsies, he was the only person they had seen thus far this morning.

'Thank you, Jenkins,' John responded. 'We will be there directly.'

'I have sent one of the servants for your trunks.'

'Very good.'

Was this the end? Lydia felt her heart pounding with the sudden realization that they were very near to quitting this place forever. Not that it was a house which had endeared itself to her during their brief stay; she would not feel any great loss at being parted from any of its inmates, but to go like this, retreating from the scene of battle, as it were . . . was not to be borne.

* * *

They rose from the table, making their way towards the front door. Nobody was there to bid them goodbye. It was not to be expected.

'Surely we should pay our respects to Miss Leverett and her mother,' Lydia ventured, standing forlornly in the middle of the hall.

'I hardly think they will expect it.' John glanced back towards the drawing-room. 'It is best not to make this any more difficult.'

'For them, or for us?'

John grunted. 'For everyone.'

They were almost at the door when a voice hallooed from the stairs, causing them to turn and look up. It was Portia, descending swiftly, her skirt almost billowing behind her. Still refusing to wear mourning, she was dressed in a round gown of Pomona green silk with an overmantle of figured muslin.

'I am so sorry,' she said breathlessly, as soon as she reached them. 'I almost missed you! But I could not let you go without thanking you for your efforts on my behalf.'

'You need not thank us, Miss Leverett,' John protested. 'We have done little enough, in all conscience.'

'It was a valiant attempt.' Her smile was also a valiant attempt at light-hearted bravado. If it did not quite succeed, it was no wonder.

'We must be going,' Lydia said, wishing now to quit this place as quickly as they were able.

'I shall accompany you to your carriage.'

'By no means,' Lydia protested.

'It is a dismal day outside.' John concurred with his wife's words. 'Quite grey and with a fine mizzle of rain.'

'No, no,' the young lady insisted, apparently determined to do her duty as a hostess. 'You cannot dissuade me. Indeed, I have already sent one of the housemaids for my cloak, so you need not fear that I shall catch a chill on your account.'

Even as she spoke, a young girl bustled up to them with a cape of bottle green draped over her extended arms. She held it out to Miss Leverett. Portia reached out to take it, then drew back suddenly.

'My dear Libby,' she said wearily, 'this is not my cloak. This belongs to my mother.'

Libby blushed a deep shade of red, much chagrined at both the mild reprimand and the realization of her mistake.

'I beg pardon, Miss Portia,' she stammered. 'But it's so like your own cloak . . . almost the same colour . . . and what with them hanging right next to each other an' all . . . '

Lydia felt her heart leap suddenly in her breast. She looked at John, finding him looking back at her. The light she saw in his eyes must surely be reflected in her own.

'John!' she cried.

'Lydia!' he echoed, stepping forward and lifting her in his arms to twirl her about in a circle right in the middle of the hall.

Miss Leverett and the little maid stared at them in amazement, clearly under the impression that they had taken leave of their senses.

'Whatever is the matter?' the former asked.

'You know, don't you?' John spoke to Lydia, quite ignoring the other two.

'I do. Oh I do, John.'

'The greatcoat!'

'Yes. But it is mad, John. Why would — ?'

'No.' he stopped her words. 'Do you not see? Miss Padgett!'

'What of Miss Padgett?' Portia demanded,

looking from one to the other, justifiably confused and more than a little suspicious of their inexplicable behaviour.

'I think Miss Padgett has known the truth all along,' he said, regaining his more placid demeanour. 'She told us both last night, but we were not listening . . . or at least, not understanding.'

Lydia struggled to grasp the thread of his thoughts, which seemed to dangle tantalizingly out of reach like the tail of a kite. What had Miss Padgett told them? What had she said? Slowly she began to remember . . .

Jenkins appeared once more, announcing that the carriage was waiting.

'Tell our driver to hold the horses,' John instructed. 'We shall not be leaving just yet. Indeed, it may be some time before we are ready to depart.'

'You are not going?' Portia remained uncomprehending.

'My dear Miss Leverett,' he said with a smile, 'do not be amazed, but my wife and I have discovered the truth about Sir Benedict's murder.'

* * *

John might command her all he dared, but still Portia could not refrain from a gasp of surprised delight at these words.

'But — but how — what . . . ' She was almost incoherent with joy. 'Are you quite certain, sir?'

'Yes.' He glanced at Lydia, for whom the final pieces were only now falling into place. 'I think I may say with confidence that I know what happened that night.'

'But only a few moments ago you expressed regret at your failure to find the truth. What has changed, sir?'

'You might say that it was the intervention of Divine Providence — and the mistake of a housemaid.'

Portia glanced at Libby, who was still standing there holding the wrong cloak, her mouth and eyes equally wide open at the strange sights and even stranger words she had just heard.

While they were thus grouped, a knock at the door heralded the arrival of Mr Kempton, who had come to call and see how Miss Padgett was getting on. He seemed to have a penchant for appearing at such moments.

'You are come in good time, sir,' John hailed him. 'I would appreciate it if you would be good enough to join us all in the drawing-room, for I have something of importance to relate to everyone.'

Baffled and more than a little hesitant, Mr

Kempton nevertheless must have decided that it was useless to argue with the large gentleman. He consented meekly, and was led to the drawing-room by Lydia herself. Portia, meanwhile, went in search of her mama and Mr Chetwin. She enquired whether she should fetch Miss Padgett, since it seemed that she was an integral part of the procedure. However, John graciously excused the ailing lady, saying that her presence was not strictly necessary. She had already played her part.

★ ★ ★

Within a very few minutes, they were all assembled — grudgingly, perhaps, but that could not be helped. Mrs Leverett complained that her nerves were in tatters, and Mr Chetwin grumbled that he thought they were done with this nonsense. John merely shrugged and stood to address them, while Lydia prepared to assist him. He was quite impressive at such moments, as she well knew. Alas, there is something about a tall man which commands the attention of an audience far more quickly and thoroughly than a slight female can hope to do.

'As you know,' John said, commencing his address with a brief preamble, 'my wife and I were asked by Miss Leverett to undertake the task of finding out who murdered her uncle, the late Sir Benedict Stanbury.'

A muffled oath from Mr Chetwin was his only response, while the others stared mutely at Mr Savidge.

'We thought it best,' Lydia picked up the tale, 'to speak with everyone concerned in the matter, which included both those residing at Fallowfield, those employed here, and anyone in Ware who might have some knowledge of the matter.'

'It has been a most perplexing and difficult affair,' John admitted, 'and we had constrained ourselves to a period of but three days in which to unravel all that we learned.'

'Until this very morning, we thought the case quite hopeless.'

'And what was it that changed your mind?' Mr Kempton could not help but ask a question to which everyone sought to know the answer.

'First,' John informed them elusively, 'let me tell you, as far as I am able, exactly what happened on the day Sir Benedict died.'

20

The Truth at Last

'You were not here the day Benedict died,' Mrs Leverett pointed out with pardonable scepticism. 'How can you pretend to know what happened?'

'Just what I was thinking, ma'am.' Mr Chetwin did not bother to disguise his own contempt.

'I have pieced together the tale from the fragments of the story told me by those with whom I've spoken,' John explained patiently. 'Like a piece of shattered porcelain, the pattern may seem to be lost, but one can reconstruct it by carefully collecting the pieces and putting them in their proper places.'

'That is all very well,' Portia said impatiently. 'But we are dealing with matters of life and death here, not a broken teapot.'

'You are right, Miss Leverett.' John inclined his head in assent. 'Now, if you will permit me, I will begin putting the pieces together;

and in the end, we will have a complete picture of the murder of Sir Benedict.'

'Get on with it, then.' Portia seated herself reluctantly.

Lydia stood beside John, facing the others, who were arranged in a half-circle, their eyes trained upon the two Savidges. They might have been a curious audience waiting to hear a fine lecturer begin his presentation.

'On the day that Sir Benedict died,' John began, 'he quarrelled with two persons. The first was Mr Kempton.'

Here, all eyes moved from John and Lydia to the poor solicitor, who sat very stiffly, vainly attempting to ignore the looks of suspicion upon the faces of his companions.

'I think we need not go into that, John,' Lydia suggested gently, with an encouraging smile at the solicitor. 'It has turned out to be much less important than we imagined.'

'I'm afraid we spent far more time looking into that quarrel than it ever warranted,' John agreed.

'And what of the other quarrel?' Mrs Leverett asked, intrigued in spite of herself.

'Ah!' John's eyes glimmered momentarily. 'That was a different matter altogether.'

He went on to describe what had transpired between the deceased gentleman and the maid, Bridget. When he mentioned that she had revealed to her master that his niece was romantically involved with one of his own servants, he could not resist a glance at Miss Leverett, who appeared perfectly unaffected and at ease. Lydia, watching the direction of his gaze, wondered what else he could have expected.

'We believe,' John continued, 'that this was the first Sir Benedict knew of Miss Leverett's association with Mr Bromley. I do not doubt that he was enraged to learn of it.'

'Who would not be!' Mr Chetwin's eyes also turned in Portia's direction, though with more malice than curiosity.

'His pride could never endure such a . . . a shocking *misalliance*,' the bereaved sister-in-law admitted.

'Quite.'

'He told no one what he had learned, however.' Lydia now took up the tale. 'Instead, he fumed in silence all day, but when everyone else had retired for the evening, he sat down to write out a new will which disinherited his niece and left the bulk of his estate to Mr Chetwin.'

'A traitorous deed!' Mrs Leverett cried, at her most dramatic. 'Was my daughter's crime so black that it merited such a cruel kind of punishment?'

'*He has an unforgiving eye,*' Lydia quoted,

'*and a damned disinheriting countenance.*'

Having uttered so crude a statement, it was now her turn to be gaped at. Mr Chetwin gave a snort of contempt and even Mr Kempton was seen to colour ever so slightly.

'The words are not mine,' Lydia hastened to reassure them, 'but Mr Sheridan's. My father took us to London to see a performance of *The School for Scandal* this past February.'

This mollified at least some of the party, for one could scarcely censure a playwright of Mr Sheridan's stature. Men of genius must be forgiven the occasional lapse in taste.

'Benedict's actions were perfectly justified, in my opinion.' This, of course, from Mr Chetwin again.

'A man certainly may do as he likes with his own money,' Mr Kempton allowed, not forgetting the great tradition of British common law.

Portia was not so easily distracted. 'This does not bring us any nearer to learning who killed my uncle.'

John began again.

'I do not think he meant to go through with it.'

'With what?' she asked.

'With disinheriting you,' Lydia answered for him, as wives are wont to do for their husbands. 'He was going to threaten you with disinheritance in order to persuade you to sever your connection with Mr Bromley.'

'He would have failed in such an attempt!' she declared, unwavering in her loyalty to the absent James.

'Naturally,' Lydia said soothingly. 'But such was, we believe, his intention.'

'He planned to confront you at the Temple of the Seven Virtues that very night,' John said. 'Bridget had already informed him that you and your lover would meet there many evenings after midnight.'

'This is all nothing but the workings of your own cork-brained imagination, Mr Savidge,' Lawrence Chetwin challenged him, his anger growing alarmingly. 'What proof do you have? And what, in any case, is your point? What does it matter what poor Benedict thought or intended? He is dead!'

'But he should not be,' John said with calm deliberation.

'Of course he should not be!' Mr Chetwin shouted back at him. 'If there were any real justice in this wicked world, it would be James Bromley buried in the churchyard at Ware!'

'Exactly so, sir.' John was apparently quite pleased at Mr Chetwin's perspicacity. 'I could not have put it better myself.'

'What!' Portia was now as incensed as Mr Chetwin had ever been. 'Do you mean to imply that you think James killed Uncle Benedict after all?'

'Oh no.' John remained as calm as ever. 'James Bromley, I am reasonably sure, has never killed anyone.'

'What then?' she demanded, perhaps pardonably confused.

Requesting their collective patience for but a few minutes longer, John returned to his tale. He commented that there were at least four persons flitting about the grounds of Fallowfield that evening: herself, James Bromley, Sir Benedict, and the killer. He dismissed the first two of these four and concentrated only upon the last two, whose footsteps he traced from house to temple.

'By the time Sir Benedict made his way to the temple,' he said at last, 'all unaware that this midnight walk would be his last, the killer was already there, waiting in the shadows . . . grimly determined on his course: which was to murder *James Bromley*.'

★ ★ ★

For several moments there was absolute silence in the drawing-room. John certainly had their full attention now.

'James Bromley!' Mrs Leverett managed to gasp out at last.

'Are you saying that *James* was the intended victim all along?' Portia cried, attempting to adjust her ideas, just as John and Lydia had been forced to do so recently.

'That is indeed what I am saying, Miss Leverett.'

'You see,' Lydia explained helpfully, 'we had been looking at this the wrong way around all the time.'

'Because Sir Benedict was the one who was shot,' John expanded upon her words, 'we assumed that he was the one who was *meant* to be killed.'

'But we always found ourselves stumbling over one apparently inescapable fact: nobody knew that Sir Benedict would be in the temple on that night.'

'But somebody *must* have known, Mrs Savidge!' Mr Kempton insisted.

'So we thought ourselves,' Lydia said sympathetically. 'It seems so natural a conclusion.'

'But it is quite wrong,' John finished her thought. 'Sir Benedict did not tell anyone of his plan.'

'There were, however, several people who knew — or at least were reasonably certain — that James Bromley would be meeting Portia there sometime shortly after midnight.'

'But it is too incredible!' Mrs Leverett

protested. 'Who, in heaven's name, would want to kill a mere stable hand?'

'It is a question we never thought to ask ourselves,' John told her, 'until we had already learned the truth.'

'In short,' Lydia said with a sly look at John, 'we knew the *who* of this matter before we had ever considered the *why* of it.'

'Still you speak in riddles.' Portia was more agitated than ever. 'For all your talk, you have not proved James innocent, or anyone else guilty. And besides which, it sounds like utter nonsense.'

'But it is not.'

'Then explain to me,' she quipped, with a raised eyebrow directed at John, 'how anyone could possibly mistake my uncle for James? One would have to be blind to — '

Suddenly she stopped, her words suspended in midsentence and her mouth forming an 'O' of belated and most unpleasant comprehension.

'Not quite blind,' Lydia said gently. 'But very nearly so.'

★　★　★

For the second time that morning there was absolute silence in the room. This time, however, every eye was turned not towards

235

John and Lydia. Instead, Lawrence Chetwin was the object of their most earnest contemplation.

'No!' Portia said, when she was able to recover her voice. 'No. It cannot be possible.'

'*You* killed Sir Benedict, Mr Chetwin.' John's words were not a suggestion but a confident assertion of truth.

Lawrence Chetwin might have been a corpse himself, so stiff and still he had become. His response to John, when it came, was spoken evenly, even flatly.

'Why would I kill the man who was closer to me than a brother — my greatest friend in the world?'

'You would never have killed Sir Benedict . . . intentionally,' Lydia answered him. 'But, as we discovered, you were there to rid yourself of someone quite different.'

'The truth is so simple,' John said, 'that it was overlooked. All our attention was directed toward Sir Benedict, when we should have asked ourselves who would want to kill James Bromley.'

'But why would Lawrence wish to kill James?' Mrs Leverett asked, still grappling with the implications of what she had heard.

John turned to Portia. 'You told us yourself, Miss Leverett, that Mr Chetwin considered himself one of the family.'

'He must have felt that you had brought dishonour to the Stanbury name by your affair with James — ' Lydia began.

'Of course she had!' Mr Chetwin himself interrupted her. 'Cavorting about with a common stable hand! It was not to be tolerated!'

'It was none of your affair, Winny,' Portia spat back.

'I think that Mr Chetwin knew something even before that day. He did not wish to burden his friend with the knowledge But that changed the moment that Bridget revealed the truth so brazenly.'

'Now the whole county is aware of it!' Mr Chetwin said in disgust. 'But I was nowhere near Benedict when he quarrelled with that little trollop, Bridget.'

'No.' John could not deny his words. 'You were in this very room with Miss Padgett. She told us so herself. She also told us that she heard voices raised in the hall but was unable to hear what was being said between Sir Benedict and the maid.'

'There!' Mr Chetwin cried triumphantly. 'Does that not prove that I knew nothing of the matter until after Benedict's death, when the whole sordid affair became common knowledge among everyone from here to Bishop's Stortford — '

'Ah!' Lydia's voice intoned that one compelling syllable. 'That was undoubtedly the impression which Miss Padgett intended to convey to us, and succeeded in doing so, too.'

'Miss Padgett is no fool,' John declared, 'unless it be considered foolish to be in love.'

'What?' Both Mr Chetwin and Miss Leverett uttered the word together.

'I believe her to be in love with you,' John said, not at all as if it were any great announcement. 'I also believe that she knows you well enough to have guessed that you were guilty of the crime. But she could not bring herself to expose you.'

'Delia?' Mr Chetwin swallowed something in his throat, but said no more.

'She was perfectly honest in saying that she had been unable to hear what passed between the two in the hall that day.' Lydia gave the gentleman a knowing look. 'But because *she* did not hear what was said, it does not necessarily follow that *you* did not.'

'I recall that I once remarked that the loss of one faculty, such as seeing, is generally compensated by the gain in another.' John paused, as if daring the other man to deny what he was saying. 'You then told me that your hearing was most acute. I do not doubt that you heard pretty much all that Bridget told Sir Benedict.'

The tale which John then unfolded to them was dark enough to keep his listeners quite entranced. No eyelid flickered, no turn of the head broke the spell as he related how Mr Chetwin's anger had led to the development of a desperate plan, which he lost little time in carrying out.

He could not allow the family honour to be besmirched in such a fashion. In his mind, only one person was responsible for what had happened: the low-born James Bromley. It followed, therefore, that James Bromley must be punished, indeed, that he must be eliminated, if they were to save themselves from further disgrace.

Sometime during the day, he had managed to steal into the study and snatch one of the pistols, probably concealing it in his bed-chamber. Knowing the hour at which the lovers generally met — as related by Bridget — he stole down the back stairs toward the kitchen door at least half an hour beforehand. If anyone had chanced to encounter him in the hall or on the stairs, he could easily have concealed his weapon and feigned some excuse for his nocturnal perambulations. He was in luck, however. Nobody else was about just then, so he descended the stairs and reached into the alcove for his greatcoat.

'And there, sir,' John said, 'you made your first mistake.'

John looked about him at the circle of eager faces.

'What mistake?' Portia asked, as he had expected.

'In his haste,' Lydia replied to her question, 'he took the wrong coat. He put on Sir Benedict's greatcoat instead of his own. Miss Leverett had already pointed out to us that they were hanging side by side in the alcove.'

Portia gasped. 'Of course! That is why my uncle was not wearing one!'

'Sir Benedict,' John continued with his tale, 'must have made his way to the hall only minutes after Mr Chetwin. Not finding his greatcoat there, he apparently chose to make his way outside clad only in the coat he had worn to supper that evening.'

'Benedict would never have put on anyone's clothes but his own.' Mrs Leverett spoke with the authority of one who had known the gentleman intimately for many years. 'He was most peculiar about such things.'

'As I thought.' In spite of himself, John could not resist a moment of self-congratulation. It passed swiftly, and he went on with his story.

'Bridget's information must have been very

precise,' he said. 'Mr Chetwin knew that the signal which the lovers employed was for James to arrive first at the temple and light a lamp which was secreted there. Miss Leverett would only join him once the lamp was lit and could be seen through the temple windows. There was no light when he arrived, so it followed that the first person who would come through the door must be the stable hand.'

Having completed his task, Mr Chetwin waited just behind the door of the temple. It never entered his mind that anyone else might be coming there that night. Why should he have supposed such a thing, after all? But Sir Benedict, spurred by the same sense of anger at his niece's outrageous behaviour, but with a very different purpose in mind, was only minutes behind him.

'Had you but waited,' — John shook his head sadly at Chetwin — 'all might have been different. Had you only paused to ascertain that the person who entered the temple was the one you were expecting, how much suffering might have been averted.'

'But you did not dare hesitate,' Lydia reminded him. 'If you did so, James Bromley might be able to overpower you before you had completed the task you had set yourself.'

'Mr Bromley, I understand, is very much

the same height as Sir Benedict was?' John glanced at Miss Leverett, who nodded assent. 'You could discern that the figure which entered was a man. It was only natural for you to assume that the man was James Bromley. The pistol was in your hand. You raised it and pointed it at the head of the person who stood little more than a yard away — '

'And the last sight which Sir Benedict ever saw in this world,' Lydia concluded dramatically, 'was the face of his dearest friend as he fired the gun which put an end to his life.'

'Damn my eyes!' Lawrence Chetwin cried, no longer able to control the emotion which gripped him. 'Damn my eyes!'

He began to weep, his body shaking with the force of his sorrow. Lydia was touched in spite of herself. Not so Portia Leverett.

'Say rather, 'Damn your infernal pride'!' she shouted. 'Had you possessed a shred of sympathy, a mite of forgiveness, you would not be sitting there now with the knowledge that *you* are responsible for the death of your friend.'

'No!' the man shouted back at her, almost demented in his grotesque combination of rage and grief. 'It was you — you and that worthless servant! But for you, Benedict would still be alive!'

21

A Victorious Departure

It was almost noon, and a change had come over Fallowfield. All was turned upside-down. Having exposed his guilt so thoroughly, there was nothing for it but to take Lawrence Chetwin away. He was even now in the gaol at Ware, and Portia Leverett was rejoicing in having her beloved James Bromley restored to her.

Portia and James were now seated side by side in the drawing-room where the momentous revelations had taken place. Mrs Leverett, still inclined to look with disfavour upon the most unsuitable young man who was soon to become her son-in-law, was so overcome by all that had happened, that she was laid up in bed and threatening to stick her spoon in the wall upon the least provocation. Mr Kempton, who had been silent through most of the proceedings, had hurried off to town to open his lips at last and deliver to all who would listen every detail that he had learned. Lydia had no doubt that by evening the whole of Hertfordshire would be acquainted with the deliciously decadent doings of the Stanbury family.

'I still cannot credit it,' Portia declared to Lydia and John, who were seated opposite. 'That Winny — *Winny*, of all people — could have done such a thing.'

'Think how much more surprised Mr Chetwin must have been when he realized that not only had he shot the wrong man, but that he had killed the person nearest to him in all the world.'

'You are right, Lydia.' The young lady turned to James Bromley, who looked somewhat sheep-faced and bewildered, as if he longed to be back in the stables rather than in the elegant drawing-room. 'I remember that night, when I ran back to the house to tell them what I had found. Winny was perfectly calm when he first saw me, though I must have looked positively wild myself.'

Only when she told them whom she had found in the temple did Mr Chetwin's countenance change so dramatically. He was, she said, as white as a lily, and he repeated over and over that she must be mistaken, it *could not be Sir Benedict.*

'Of course.' John leaned back in his chair. 'In *his* mind, he had shot Mr Bromley.

Anything else was incomprehensible.'

'Now that I think of it,' Lydia said, half to herself and half to James, 'Mr Chetwin never actually accused you of shooting his friend. Whenever he spoke of it, he said that you were *responsible* for Sir Benedict's death, and that he would still be alive were it not for *you*.'

'He considered himself quite blameless, you know.' John ruminated on the tenor of Mr Chetwin's character. 'So far as he was concerned, he had merely been attempting to right a wrong — a wrong done by Miss Leverett and Mr Bromley.'

'It seemed to him only right and proper that you should suffer for the crime, since it would never have happened without your interference, so to speak. He had failed to rid himself of you, but the hangman would accomplish his purpose for him.'

'How wicked!' Portia cried.

Lydia agreed with her. 'The miracle is that you never saw him in the park that night.'

'Not such a miracle.' Portia shrugged. 'Winny knows every tree and shrub on the estate, I'll wager. He knew which path I was likely to take, and skirted around it.'

'Then he came back to the house, returned the coat to its place in the alcove, and slipped up the back stairs and to his bedchamber without anyone being the wiser.'

It was probably mere minutes afterwards that Portia arrived with the news which turned out to be as much of a shock to him as to anyone.

'I think I know his feelings,' James said, with a degree of Christian charity which Lydia was forced to acknowledge that she could not emulate. 'He acted in accordance with his conscience, if he thought me more guilty than him.'

'But he was wrong,' his beloved insisted.

'Indeed he was,' Lydia seconded her statement.

'I believe that if anyone had actually asked him whether he had fired the shot which killed Sir Benedict,' John suggested, his face grave, 'he would have confessed immediately. His sense of honour would not have allowed him to actually lie about it. He did not consider that he had *killed* him, but rather that he merely shot him.'

'But nobody ever thought to put such a question to him,' Lydia said, stating the obvious. 'It was too fantastic a supposition.'

'I cannot thank you enough for what you have done.' Portia's words were directed at both of them.

'We came very close to failure, my dear Miss Leverett,' John admitted. 'But for the mistake with your cloak, we might even now be on our way back to Diddlington, and Mr Bromley would still be a prisoner.'

The fact remained, however, that Lydia's prayers for a sign had been answered in the most unlikely manner. In the end, Portia did not know which of them deserved the most thanks. Lydia suggested that she might, perhaps, reserve her thanks for God; but Portia was not at present very well acquainted with the Deity, though she could hardly refuse such a request. James, somewhat more orthodox in his views, was happy to do as they asked.

In the end, it was Portia's hand raised to wave goodbye to them as their carriage finally pulled away down the drive. James, whose situation and character both demanded that he be more subdued, merely smiled his gratitude and watched as they disappeared into the distance.

★   ★   ★

'I must say that I am not sorry to see the last of this place,' Lydia confessed to John as they turned the bend in the road which removed Fallowfield from their sight.

'You have not enjoyed this murder as much as the last, my dear?' he quipped.

'Portia is a girl of great spirit and determination,' she said, willing herself to be generous.

'But she is a hoyden of whom one grows weary very quickly.' John folded his arms and looked directly at his wife. 'Said I not so?'

'You did.' Her words were spoken grudgingly. 'But indeed the inhabitants at Fallowfield are the kind of people for whom it is impossible to feel any great affection.'

'Most of them hardly need it,' he observed, 'as they all have such overweening affection for themselves.'

'The only one with whom I can truly sympathize is poor Miss Padgett.'

'She is a truly tragic figure.'

'She has lost the man she loves.'

'I fear so.'

'And she is now forced to spend her life in the company of two women who are likely to drive her to distraction.'

'They will not throw her out to fend for herself,' John said judiciously.

Lydia sighed. 'It might almost be better for her if they did.'

'She is too sensible not to realize that her fate might be far worse.'

'Do you think that anything *could* be worse?'

'I think that rather than contemplating the

woes of Miss Padgett, you had better instead celebrate the success of Mr and Mrs Savidge.'

'We have helped to save the life of yet another innocent man.' Her eyes brightened.

'And was that not precisely what we set out to do?'

'So it was.'

'Your papa would be very proud,' he asserted.

'Of his daughter *and* his son-in-law.'

'So we may now return home with our self-esteem enlarged and our heads held high.'

'Noses in the air!' she cried gaily.

'And a tale to tell which I'm afraid will not gladden the heart of Mrs Wardle-Penfield.'

EPILOGUE

Home again

Mr and Mrs John Savidge were now firmly established in Bellefleur, their absurdly large house near the village of Diddlington in Sussex. Their honeymoon had provided an adventure which few newlywed couples generally experience, but now all was peace and contentment . . . or nearly so.

Neither of them was used to living in such magnificence, nor in a pile as grand and ornate as the ancient mansion. It was almost time for them to attend the wedding of Lydia's sister, Louisa, which event was to be celebrated at St Clement's in London. Since her aunt and uncle, the Comte and Comtesse d'Almain, were to accompany them to town for the occasion, Lydia had suddenly been inspired to extend to them a more generous invitation: to come and live with them at Bellefleur.

John was quite as enthusiastic as she could have wished. After all, their lives were already inextricably linked ever since they had cleared the good name of the *comte* and helped clear his path to the altar with the former Camilla Denton.

The older couple, both touched and surprised at the notion, promised to consider it most seriously. Both John and Lydia accepted it as settled then. It was a most sensible arrangement. The distinguished French nobleman was far more accustomed to such a palatial residence, and the small cottage in which he and his new bride now lived could be let in order to increase their modest income. In spite of the fact that Mr and Mrs d'Almain were hampered by possessing the most romantic of dispositions, their capitulation seemed quite inevitable.

Meanwhile, they had to make arrangements for their journey up to London, a place which Aunt Camilla, for her part, had never even seen. Lydia was discussing with John what clothes they should carry with them, and precisely how long they were likely to be there, when they were interrupted by the arrival of a visitor who needed no introduction to either of them.

'Well!' A penetrating voice proclaimed the identity of this very important person even before she came into view. 'I declare I am abashed beyond all measure.'

'You truly do not look it, Mrs P,' John greeted the great lady saucily. 'You appear quite *au fait*, as always.'

'Good morning to you, John . . . Lydia,' she returned crisply, hauling her ample frame over to a convenient chair, where John seated her with great ceremony. 'I have just this instant received a letter from . . . from Fallowfield . . . and came at once to acquaint you with the latest news from that Mansion of Vice.'

'Is it another murder?' Lydia suggested hopefully.

'Worse than that.'

Even Lydia was startled by this. 'Whatever can it be?'

Mrs Wardle-Penfield adjusted the ribbons of her bonnet, then removed the sheet of crossed paper from her reticule and held it before her, apparently needing to peruse it once more in order to ascertain that her eyes had not deceived her the first time.

'Portia,' she declared at last, 'has married her stable hand, against the wishes of all her family. Not,' she added bitterly, 'that she had much choice in the matter. Their . . . their *love-child* (for one can call it no better) is to be born in the spring.'

'I wish her all possible happiness,' Lydia said sincerely.

'With that common servant?' Mrs Wardle-Penfield was scandalized.

Both Lydia and John privately thought that Miss Leverett was getting the best of the bargain, but wisely refrained from saying so.

'I would not dismiss Mr Bromley so quickly, ma'am,' was all John remarked. It was enough, however, to arrest the old woman in mid-tirade.

'Why not?'

'I have made certain enquiries concerning the drawings which Miss Leverett showed me, and they have been examined by a member of the Royal Academy, where it seems Mr Bromley will soon be going to study under some of our foremost artists.'

'A painter!' Mrs Wardle-Penfield snorted her disgust. 'That my own godchild should ally herself to a mere drawing-master, which is only slightly more acceptable than a stable hand.'

'I think young James will distinguish himself someday, and be more highly regarded than you might now imagine.'

'Very true.' Her response was crisp and negative. 'My imagination cannot stretch to such incredible heights as that.'

'That is a great pity,' Lydia said demurely. Of course anything as demure as that was wasted upon this grand dame.

'And to think that we had such high hopes — her mother and I — that she would marry Sir Caleb Hovington. But it seems,' she continued, with deep regret, 'that he now has some high-flier in keeping. She is actually an acquaintance of Portia: just the kind of female she *would* be acquainted with, from what I can gather.'

'Bridget!' John and Lydia exclaimed in unison.

'I believe you are correct. That is her name — at least I believe it is, for the writing is barely more than a scrawl.' She frowned at them, not so pleased at their own apparent knowledge of this less than respectable person.

'That, at least, is a most appropriate match,' Lydia said with a glance at John.

'I have been quite deceived in Portia,' Mrs Wardle-Penfield pronounced, as one about to consign someone to perdition. 'And as for her *mother*! . . . Ah well,' she concluded, her sudden passion dying down to mild disgust, 'now that I recall, Pamela always was rather bird-witted. Nice enough gel, but not of the very best sort. Perhaps I should not have expected any more from her daughter.'

'You have been most unfortunate in your goddaughter, ma'am,' John was all mock-sympathy.

'Yes,' she agreed, insensible to irony. 'I must see if I can do better for myself.'

'Indeed.'

She fixed her gaze earnestly upon Lydia, who felt a certain foreboding.

'I shall be godmother to your first child, Lydia,' Mrs Wardle-Penfield announced. As usual with her, it was not a suggestion, but a decree. 'You will no doubt be increasing soon enough, and I am sure you cannot do worse by your offspring than Pamela has done by hers.'

'You are too kind.'

Lydia knew not whether to laugh or cry. She feared she might be in danger of both. Nobody else, she reflected, would think of appointing themselves to such a position without so much as a hint from the parents of the poor, unsuspecting infant, who, in this case, had not yet been conceived.

'Well, I had better leave you to it.'

The older woman stood up, apparently having decided that Lydia and John would set about conceiving their first child the moment her back was turned.

'Very well, then.'

'I understand that your aunt and the Frenchman are coming to live here at Bellefleur with you.' She paused by the door, throwing this remark casually over her shoulder. How the deuce did she know about that?

'We have considered such a possibility, yes.'

'In general I do not hold with such arrangements,' she said. 'However, in this case I think it is very sensible of you. Camilla needs taking care of, and at least you will be too busy to be getting mixed up in any more murders.'

'Oh, we have quite given up on murder, ma'am,' John assured her.

'I am glad to hear it.'

'But then again,' Lydia added wickedly, 'one never knows.'

'What!'

Lydia smiled up at her.

'It is just possible,' she pointed out, 'that murder has not yet given up on *us*.'

We do hope that you have enjoyed reading this large print book.

Did you know that all of our titles are available for purchase?

We publish a wide range of high quality large print books including:
Romances, Mysteries, Classics
General Fiction
Non Fiction and Westerns

Special interest titles available in large print are:
The Little Oxford Dictionary
Music Book
Song Book
Hymn Book
Service Book

Also available from us courtesy of Oxford University Press:
Young Readers' Dictionary
(large print edition)
Young Readers' Thesaurus
(large print edition)

For further information or a free brochure, please contact us at:
Ulverscroft Large Print Books Ltd.,
The Green, Bradgate Road, Anstey,
Leicester, LE7 7FU, England.
Tel: (00 44) 0116 236 4325
Fax: (00 44) 0116 234 0205

Other titles published by
The House of Ulverscroft:

HIDDEN IN THE HEART

Beth Andrews

While her pretty older sister Louisa is being presented to London Society for the season, Lydia Bramwell is sent to her Aunt Camilla in Sussex. High-spirited Lydia expects a dull visit, but the village of Diddlington is not the tranquil idyll she anticipates. When a charred and bludgeoned corpse is found in the woods nearby, suspicion falls on Camilla's suitor, a handsome Frenchman. Convinced of his innocence, Lydia is helped by her new friend, John Savidge, to catch the real killer. But before their dangerous adventure ends there will be more than one unexpected discovery.

THE UNKNOWN

James Pattinson

Mrs Craydon was taken with the idea of digging up the history of the family. And once started she became more enchanted by the project. Even her husband George, having once seen the ancient photograph of a most attractive girl, long since dead, developed an interest in the family genealogy. The only snag was that even Great-Aunt Maud, the owner of the photograph, had no idea what had happened to the beautiful girl named Isabella. Apparently she had completely vanished and to the rest of the family had simply become The Unknown. Would the mystery ever be solved?

GALLOWS LANE

Brian McGilloway

In the Irish borderlands a series of gruesome murders takes place. Garda Inspector Benedict Devlin's enquiries point to a local body builder, but then born-again ex-con James Kerr is found nailed to a tree — crucified. Devlin realizes that the case is more complex, and more sinister, than he had imagined. Meanwhile, as Devlin's relationships with his colleagues on both sides of the border become fraught, the body count rises, and he's suddenly fighting for more than the truth. Now Devlin's determination to apprehend the culprit — or culprits — before they strike again, starts to jeopardize those he cares about most.

THE WIG MAKER

Roger Silverwood

Wig maker Peter Wolff is found dead and his workshop on fire. There are no clues, no DNA and no motive — Detective Inspector Michael Angel is baffled. At the same time, high-flying model Katrina Chancey goes missing; womanizer Gabriel Grainger is reported missing by his wife Zoë; Lord Tiverton has been robbed of a suit of armour; jewel robberies by The Fox continue unabated, and another body is discovered in unexpected circumstances. Now, using all his skills, and applying his unique quirkiness, Inspector Angel must race to the finish to find the murderer, and solve all the mysteries.

THE BODY IN THE SNOWDRIFT

Katherine Hall Page

Faith Fairchild's father-in-law celebrates his seventieth birthday by taking the entire family for a week-long stay at the Pine Slopes ski resort. All starts well until Faith discovers a body on a cross-country trail, and Pine Slopes' star chef vanishes without a trace. One catastrophe follows another: a malicious prank, a break-in at the Fairchilds' condo and the sabotage of one of the chairlifts. There is also a mysterious woman living in the woods — and Faith's nephew Scott, and Ophelia Stafford, are up to something . . . Family secrets abound as Faith struggles to salvage the reunion . . . and save her own life.